SHAKEN

LIFE AS WE KNEW IT

Shaken

Life As We Knew It

Felice S.C

For information, kindly email the author
feliciacauley@ymail.com.
rightsideceo@yahoo.com
www.rightsidepiblishing.com

Right Side Publishing P. O Box 339 Reynoldsburg, Ohio 43068
please note address may change

ISBN- 978-1-955050-15-9
LCCN- 2023903715
Published in the United States
Project manager Robert Cauley
Editor: M.O Blessing
Editor: Felicia S. Cauley
Editor: Ayesha E. B.
Editor: Mohsin

Acknowledgment

I thank God for my gift of writing and my husband Robert, our children, and extended family for their unwavering support. Special thanks to M.O Blessing, whose meticulous work on the manuscript truly invigorated this story. May the Lord Jesus Christ always bless you and your loved ones.

In these times, a story like this is what people need because everyone is drifting apart from their faith due to the allure of disbelief. Through its storytelling, the book beautifully illustrates the trials faced by believers. How this world has the tendency to take over our thoughts.

The character that truly stood out for me was Kirk; the way he was concerned for his family, always trying to provide and protect them. He went through so much, but nothing could shake his faith in God in the end. We get to learn so much from him!

It's truly an eye-opening story that shows us how deeply drowned we are in our worldly desires. It makes you realize what your priorities should be and where you stand with your faith.

Ayesha E.B

Dedication

This is for all of those who believe, are preparing, and waiting for Christ's return.

But of that day and hour knoweth no man, no, not the angels of heaven, but my Father only

Michaelhew 24:36
KJV

Table of Contents

Acknowledgment..iv

Dedication...vi

Introduction...viii

Chapter One..1

Chapter Two..13

Chapter Three..17

Chapter Four...27

Chapter Five...33

Chapter Five...47

Chapter Six..71

Chapter Seven..77

Chapter Eight..97

Chapter nine...103

Chapter Ten..107

Chapter Eleven...117

Chapter Thirteen...125

Chapter Fourteen...137

Chapter Fifteen..143

Introduction

In the serene landscapes of North Carolina, life once thrived in harmony until the ominous shadows of an approaching apocalypse loomed over the horizon. Amidst the encroaching darkness, Laura and Kirk, an expectant couple, found themselves navigating a treacherous journey beset by catastrophic events. As turmoil engulfed their world, their unwavering determination to weather the storm faltered against the relentless onslaught of fate.

With Laura's pregnancy shadowed by the impending catastrophe, their resolve and faith in God were put to the ultimate test. Tragedies mounted, instilling fear and despair, compelling people to retreat into isolation. The closure of major institutions forced the government's intervention, implanting electronic chips as a means of control. However, activating the chip came with a cost. Would anyone stake their entire living just for worldly riches?

People stopped going to church and stepping outside of their homes, banks were closed, hospitals were unavailable, and food supplies started running short. Natural disasters cascaded, intensifying the chaos until the arrival of a phenomenon reminiscent of the biblical event—"Rapture"— plunged humanity into uncertainty.

As Kirk grappled with the daunting responsibility of protecting his family, he sought aid from a friend. Yet, despite the dire circumstances, he remained steadfast in his determination to secure supplies and resources. Meanwhile, Laura battled an escalating whirlwind of emotional turmoil, torn between faith and desolation, as their trials mounted relentlessly.

Things might never go back to normal, maybe they would never live happily again, or maybe they could never step inside their home again. What else could take control of their remaining last bit of sanity?

The relentless onslaught of calamities pushed them to the brink, forcing an exodus from their homes as a government directive mandated the abandonment of Earth. One after the other, calamities affected them and hope waned, Laura's faith wavered, consumed by anger and sorrow when she experienced early labor-induced pain. However, the chaos was eased as Jenny, a midwife, and others stood by them, striving to keep their unity and faith intact.

As news of a new Messiah, Ultimo, surfaced, promising relief from suffering, tensions escalated. Refusing to yield to this new belief, a risky escape plan was forged with the help of a trusted ally. In a desperate bid for survival, they embarked on a perilous journey towards an underground bunker, where the fragility of life became starkly evident.

Tragedy struck in the confines of the bunker. Faced with a demand to surrender to Ultimo or choose death. Kirk, and his faith, chose a path that led to martyrdom, finding solace in reunion with his departed loved ones through his unwavering devotion to Christ.

Chapter One

In a small town of North Carolina, Laura and Kirk lived peacefully with their three children, Miranda, Michael, and James. Miranda was a sixteen-year-old Blessed High School International student. It was one of the best schools in the countryside with skilled teachers, excellent students, and an impressive educational environment.

Miranda sat worried after her Algebra and English tests because she thought she had not performed well in either of them. She looked up at the clock in her classroom *"2:35 pm,"* she said to herself *"Great, just one more hour left until this bell rings."*

Just then, Mr. Roberts, their Algebra and English teacher walked in holding a bulk of papers and the classroom went quiet again. Mr. Roberts was not someone who appeared to be aesthetically appealing, he seemed to be losing all hair in the middle of his head and had a regular accessory he wore on his face instead of a smile, a frown, he was very rotund and wore glasses, he had a protruded belly that always sat on his belts whenever he wore trousers.

He looked down at the students as he adjusted his glasses and he placed the papers on the central desk in the classroom, he cleared his throat as he started speaking, he also had a southern accent, "Very well now, you all should know already, what I have with me here", he said as he looked over to the students awaiting a response and the students all echoed in unison; "yes, sir", he nodded as he pranced towards the desk to pick up the papers and he began to share them amongst the students.

When he got to Miranda, he looked through her paper, he shook his head as he gave her the papers "Your performance was not very impressive, Miranda, keep this up and you may have to repeat the classes," he said as he gave her a light pat on her shoulders. She was not surprised as she expected him to say something as she collected the papers, she looked up to the side of the papers where Mr. Roberts had written the grades when she saw the letter 'D' respectively on both papers.

She bent her head over in disappointment and looked up to examine the papers again. Mr. Roberts was right, if she didn't work on improving her grades, there was a very high possibility that she would have to repeat her current class. She used the back of her hand to wipe off beads of sweat dripping from her forehead due to the tension as she was waiting to collect her test scores, "what am I going to do now, I cannot repeat the class, it is going to be hard for me to start all over again."

Mr. Robert's loud clap brought her back to reality as he made his way to the front of the class and started making the announcement, "I would like to commend a few students in the class who performed excellently well in the tests that I just conducted, if you hear your names please stand and the rest of the class, please do well to acknowledge them", he said as he reached into his pocket for a small piece of paper, he cupped his hand over his mouth as he started and cleared his throat again as he started talking.

"Michael Brown, Winter, Tom Dominique, Kim Kramer, Ronald Burkley, and Lisa Barnes", he said as he folded the paper and the class erupted in loud applause which was later cut short by the sound of Mr. Robert's voice yet again, "Now, while these students you have just applauded did excellently well, some of you did not appease me", the class became very quiet this time because they knew what he was about to do, just like he publicly acknowledged the students that did very well in the test, he was about to call out the names of the students that didn't do very well or as he expected in the test.

"When you hear your names, please stand…Anita Carleton, Miranda Grady, James Carleton, Lauren Rennes, and David Burrow", Mirada hesitated at first when she heard her name being called out and then Mr. Roberts looked down at her with furrowed brows and his folded arms, "Miranda…", Miranda looked around the class and saw all the students staring at her and she slowly stood up, *so mean*, she said to herself as she stood up to join the rest of the students that were standing after their names were called out.

"You all must do much better than you have in these tests if you want to graduate next fall, you cannot afford any further slip-ups or discrepancies in your grades from now henceforth. If you need any assistance with any of the topics that we have discussed this session, you can come to me to assist you with anything that you do not understand, I would love to help you with that, or you can go ahead and meet any of the students you feel have a vast knowledge about any topics that you may be having difficulties with, on that note, that would be…", just then the school bell rang and all the students jumped up in excitement. Mr. Robert stood up, adjusting his suit, and walking out, following him students also made their way to leave the classroom.

The ride home from school was an extremely long one, a ride that usually took about fifteen minutes became something that felt like an hour-long ride. She laid her head on the bus window and went deep into her thoughts, what had happened in school and with Mr. Roberts was starting to take a toll on her, she had never been so embarrassed until today. She certainly was not ready to face her parents, she had been struggling for a while to catch up with her studies and her bad results from the Algebra and English tests she just had were more like a wake-up call for her and she did not want to have any further issues.

The sound of the bus came to a screeching halt as she lifted her head up to look outside when she realized that the bus had just stopped on the street leading up to her house and the driver gestured for her to get off the bus. As Miranda walked down the street, she kept thinking about how she was going to tell her parents, especially her mom about yet another failure on her tests.

She walked to the front door of the house expecting to meet her mom's usual and extremely timely bear hug, but that was not the case today. Miranda walked into her house and met her mom standing by the couch next to her younger brother James; her mom had bright red curly hair with a full fringe and light freckles spread on her nose, she was of average height with big blue eyes that lit up anytime she smiled. Her younger brother James was five years old, and he seemed to have already inherited their mom's freckles but had darker hair than her. Her dad was sitting on the couch, he was slim and tall, with a head full of jet-black hair and had the shiniest brown skin. On this particular day, she was not met with smiles or pleasantries which usually made her feel welcome after a horrible day in school.

Laura had her hands on her belly, she was already four months pregnant, but the look on her face was not the one she usually had when Miranda came home from school. This look was different, it was somewhat pensive, and it made Miranda extremely jealous. Her dad looked over at her while sitting on the couch and smiled briefly at her, "Hi, Girl," he said as he gestured for her to come and join them.

Miranda returned the brief smile with a smirk on her face and went over to join them. As she sat down, placing her bag by the corner of the couch, she noticed something strange, the news channel was on; they never got around to watching the news because according to her Mom, ninety percent of the news was always bad and she did not want to raise her children to normalize feeding off negativity.

"What is going on?" Miranda asked as she settled on the couch.

Her mother stroked her belly and let out a huge sigh as she spoke, "This is why I never watch the news, there is always something bad to look forward to."

"What do you mean?" Miranda asked while looking at her mom and dad. If anything, she was glad that they were having another conversation rather than discussing her education, she wanted to stay on the topic at hand.

"Laura, don't scare the girl, eh…there is no cause for alarm, apparently this news lady…", Kirk said as he gestured to the television showing a female broadcaster, he was still trying to gather his words and he turned to her again, "the news lady says there is a prediction that an asteroid is going to hit the moon…". Before he could complete his statement, Miranda's younger brother James cut him short, "What does that mean Daddy?" he said while looking up at Kirk.

Kirk stroked his hair as he replied, "Well, it just means that you get to see something fun."

"What is something fun?" James asked again.

"Well…we'll never know until we see it, okay?"

James nodded as he replied, "Alright, Daddy," he stood up and went over to his mother, and he held her hands together while looking at her, "Mom…there is no need to worry, everything is going to be fine, okay?"

Laura smiled as she pulled him into one of her signature bear hugs, "You just know how to say the best things," she said as she smiled broadly at him.

"Do you want a milkshake or a smoothie?" Laura said as she bent over slowly to meet James's eyes.

"I…I want a smoothie milkshake," James replied.

Laura fixed her fringe and stopped it from covering her face as she burst out laughing, then stopped to catch her breath as she stroked James's hair, "Well…you can't have both baby, it's either you have a milkshake or you have a smoothie, so which one is it going to be?"

"Okay…" James responded, sounding disappointed, "I want to have a smoothie."

Laura smiled briefly as she looked at him, "So what fruits do you want in your smoothie…do you want berries, bananas, pineapples… huh, what do you want?"

James smiled and started jumping excitedly, "I want it all, I want it all, I want all of it mama!"

Laura laughed loudly and paused to catch her breath as she placed her hands on her rounded belly, she tried to pick him up but stopped almost immediately, "ooh, you have gotten really big, you funny boy," she said as she moved to tickle him, he loved being tickled.

James let out a loud giggle as Laura tickled him and proceeded to rub his hair.

"Say what…you want to help mama make your smoothie," Laura asked while she started moving towards the kitchen.

James nodded as Laura took his hand and led him to the kitchen.

Kirk turned over to Miranda and smiled, they were the only ones left in the room. At this point, Miranda started becoming frantic as she did not know what to expect, she was hoping that he was not going to ask her about school. *Please do not ask me about the school, ask me about anything but school, I will have an answer for anything else that you ask me,"* she said to herself as if she had been hoping for her father to hear her thoughts.

"So…how was school?" Kirk looked at her while waiting for her to respond.

"*Oh, just great…,"* Miranda said to herself while she was struggling to find the words, she was going to use to answer his question.

The next thing she heard was a sharp snap, her dad snapped his fingers at her, she had been lost in thought for a never-ending cycle.

"School was…," Miranda struggled to find the words as she looked up at her father wondering why she could not complete the sentence.

"Did you have a great day at school today?" Kirk said as he looked at Miranda.

"Ummm…. "Uhmmm" Miranda muttered and clasped her fingers together as she tried to figure out what to say.

"*Oh snap… Miranda, you can do this, just tell him everything that is going on right now at school, his reaction can't be that bad, right?*" she said within herself, if only those words could come out as she had said them to herself.

"Is anything the Michaeler?" Kirk asked as he tried to get her attention, "you seem so lost in your thoughts".

"Everything…everything is fine, Dad," Miranda replied while wiping some beads of sweat off her forehead, she had been extremely nervous all day.

"Okay, but just know that if you need anything at all if you need to talk to someone about anything at all, I am here for you, you can absolutely come to me if you need anything", Kirk said while he patted her gently on her shoulders and while raising his eyebrows in a bid to reaffirm everything that he just said.

"Dad, I already told you, you have absolutely nothing to worry about, I am very fine," Miranda replied with an exaggerated tone.

Just then, Laura returned from the kitchen, with James jumping with excitement as he held his cup of goodness, his cup of smoothie fruits.

Miranda heaved a sigh of relief as she looked over at them and then gestured to James with a broad smile, "you happy now?" she asked as she locked eyes with him.

James replied with an even broader smile than Miranda's, "I am very happy."

Laura looked at both James and Miranda as she hurriedly sat on the couch next to their dad, slightly stroking the small of her back and propping up the huge pillow on the couch for comfort as she laid her back on it.

"I almost lost it in there, this young man…", she said while making a face at James who giggled after he saw her face, "has a huge appetite, he almost finished up all the fruits before I could even get to blending them", she said as she raised her hands in the air.

Kirk let out a loud laugh that echoed around the room, "That's my boy."

Miranda let out a sigh and briefly rolled her eyes as she responded, "He sure is…now, what do we want to have for dinner? Mashed potatoes and carrot sauce, macaroni and steak, pork chops?" she asked while looking at their faces while waiting for them to respond so she could begin the process of getting dinner ready. Before anyone spoke up, the doorbell rang, Kirk gestured to Miranda while tilting his head to the side, "Miranda, why don't you go and see who is at the door."

Miranda nodded as she replied, "Alright Dad, I will." She went over to the front door to check and saw their neighbor, Marie Johnson, standing outside with a large pot of pie, it seemed like she had just finished baking them. She looked over at Kirk and Laura before coming into the house and she smiled, "I brought pies," she said as she began making her way into the house.

Maria was the closest friend Laura had in the neighborhood. Everyone often saw Laura as a rude, shy, or snobbish person, but in truth she was more of an introverted person, keeping to herself and this made it quite challenging to make friends, so every time she had a friend, she trusted them to a reasonable level.

Kirk laughed as Marie made her way into the living room and

hurriedly gave Laura a hug. She was still standing as she gestured to Miranda, "These are hot, be careful while you are holding them, okay?" Miranda nodded in response, "Please take them into your kitchen," she said while handing the pan of pies over to her, "Alright, Aunt Marie," Miranda said as she walked to the kitchen.

"So, how are my second favorite people in the world doing?" Marie said as she went to sit across from Kirk and Laura.

Laura was in a state of awe, and she buried her head in surprise as she looked over at Marie.

Marie noticed the expression on Laura's face and stopped at once while trying to continue the conversation, 'What is it?" she asked while looking over at Laura waiting for her to respond.

"You are just unbelievable; how did you know I was craving pies? I was going to make them myself later," Laura said.

Marie chuckled as she reached over to a side stool beside her for a napkin to clean her hands, "well, blame it on my sixth sense and the fact that I love you all too much", Kirk burst out laughing again as he looked at Marie, "You are something else!" he exclaimed as he looked over to Laura who winked slightly and raised her eyebrows in agreement with Kirk.

"So, did you guys watch the news?" Marie asked while folding the napkin back in place and putting it on a side stool.

Both sighed as they looked at Marie, Laura was trying so hard to hide her disappointment, but she failed, "these new channels never have anything good to say, it is a waste of time listening to them or buying into anything they have told you."

"Yeah…but you saw it yourself, that was the only thing that basically, all the news channels and outlets reported throughout today, so I'm starting to feel like it is a big deal," Kirk said as he replied to Laura.

"And…if all they have reported is about this asteroid coming to earth, then I am so looking forward to it," Marie said while she signaled to Laura who at this point was starting to get uninterested in the conversation.

Marie continued the conversation in a bid to appease Miranda, "I mean if you look at it, think of it this way…it has never happened before in the history of…earth!" she said while making a mental picture of the earth's rounded shape while gesturing with her hands. "It is definitely something that I am looking forward to," she said as she smiled back at Laura.

"Now what does Lance think about all this?" Laura asked, referring to Marie's husband.

"OH…you know Lance, always looking forward to a new experience and a new adventure, just like me!" she said as she yelped in excitement, "it's no wonder why I married that fine man," she continued as her eyes lit up in excitement.

"Well, as for me," Laura stopped as her hands went to her belly as she let out a small sound, she just felt the baby move for the second time today she pulled Kirk's hands to her belly as she spoke, "Did you feel that?" She asked as Kirk nodded in response with a very wide smile. Laura continued while looking over to Marie, "As for me and this baby…," she said while gently caressing her bump, "we do not believe any of it."

"Well, I think I'm with Kirk on this one, there is a high possibility that what they have said will happen. I mean they are accurate at least seventy percent of the time, so I think I'm going to take their word for it. Lance and I will be going shopping tomorrow, it's best we fully prepare for what is coming, are you guys coming? When do you want to go shopping?" Marie said as she stood up from the chair and gestured for a hug from Laura.

Laura smiled as she gently stood up from her seat while cradling her baby bump and went over to hug Marie, "Well, I'm thinking maybe we should go shopping tomorrow as well, we are going to join you," she said smilingly.

"Alright then, we will see you tomorrow," Marie responded as she made her way out of the living room.

The next morning, both families took a trip to the town's biggest store to shop for some groceries and home supplies. They could not believe the crowd they met at the storefront. Marie stopped a middle-aged man coming out of the store. "Excuse me," she said trying to get his attention, "Good day, I just wanted to ask…what is going on?" The man smiled as he responded, "I'm afraid ma'am, the store is already empty, most people came here overnight for shopping and maxed out the store. I was one of the few who were able to get some of the supplies left," Laura cupped her mouth with her right hand in disbelief.

"I hear that you can get some supplies in Parkwood church and two other stores very far away from here, you better drive down to Parkwood church before all their supplies run out," the man said, and Marie thanked him as he left. They all went back to their car and started driving to Parkwood church, on getting there they were stunned by how quickly people also joined them. Lance dreamt the night before that everyone he ran into had some kind of hard knots on their foreheads, he stopped to examine himself. Marie, Kirk, and Laura stopped and noticed hard knots had appeared on their foreheads too, this got them scared and worried.

Chapter Two

The previous day's incident got everyone worried, and a small fraction of the people in North Carolina began to prepare themselves for the worst things to happen. Laura turned to her side when she heard the alarm ring for the third time. She read the timer of the clock as she struggled to find a balance while she was on the bed, *"8:20 am"*, she looked around for any sign of sunlight and saw that it was still as dark as it was the day before when they all went to bed frantic.

She reached out for the side mirror beside their bed and lightly stroked her forehead as she examined herself with the mirror, she stopped midway there was no hard knot in the middle of her forehead. Everything that happened the day before was still hazy, she found it hard to remember some of the things that happened and struggled to regain consciousness. She looked at Kirk and saw he didn't have a knot in the middle of his forehead, her eyes lit up as she let out a soft gasp, "Oh, we do not have chips on our foreheads like Lance dreamed, I don't think this is something that will be forced on us." She said as she slowly snapped her fingers.

"Kirk…Kirk," she said softly while tapping her husband gently on the back trying to wake him up. Kirk slowly turned over to meet her eyes as he stretched his hands in the air, he gently rubbed his eyes as he opened them, "Hey baby, morning," he said as he gave her a sleepy wink and smiled. He moved to give her a soft kiss on her cheek, it seemed like she was upset about something.

"What is it?" He asked while holding her hand, Laura reached over to grab the alarm clock and she handed it over to him. He laughed as he took the alarm clock from her, "what now? Is the alarm clock broken or what?" He said while trying to examine the alarm clock to find a possible fault. Laura responded sharply as she raised her eyebrows, "Take a look at the time," Kirk nodded as he looked at the alarm clock and read the time out loud, "8:46 am", he did not understand what she meant.

Laura let out a loud grunt as she struggled to get up from the bed and walked briskly to the other side of the room and opened the curtains. "Take a look at this!" she said while pointing outside, Kirk got confused and said, "It's still very early babe, seems like this alarm clock is broken. I am going to fix it so do not worry about it, I'll get to fixing it right away".

At this point, Laura was over Kirk's impossible ignorance, she went over to him and sat by his side, "Something is definitely up, I can feel it', she said as she reached for her phone to look at the time, "8:52 am", she read out loud as she showed it to Kirk. He jerked up from bed, "I don't understand, how is it so dark when it's already morning? What does that mean?" he asked as he scrambled around the room in search of his phone. He saw that he had gotten many missed calls from some of his friends, "I think we need to head out," he said as he went over to Laura to help her stand.

They walked out of their bedroom to check on Miranda and James before leaving and saw them fast asleep. They held each other and walked quietly out of the house. As they reached the front porch, Lance saw them and made his way towards them.

"What is going on?" Kirk asked as he shook hands with Lance. It looked like he hadn't slept for hours, "after what happened yesterday...", he said pointing at his forehead and referring to the chips they all had on now, "Marie and I just wanted to have a good night's rest, but then we woke up this morning just like the rest of the people here", he said as he pointed at the people that had filled up the streets consumed with different feelings regarding the situation, "...and then we saw this", he said as he looked up to the sky which was covered in thick clouds.

Just then, the mega speakers, who were placed in different corners of the town started to make an announcement addressed by the mayor himself, "Dear people of North Carolina, it is new what we are currently going through, while it may seem as something that is very strange and unprecedented, I want to urge you all to be of good faith. I also want to tell you that this is a phase that will soon pass, while we go through this. I will ensure that the citizens are properly cared for and if anyone may need any assistance, they can reach out to the government office and be rest assured that they will get a prompt response, in all, we will always stand tall," and then the speakers went off.

Chapter Three

The last few days had been very overwhelming for everyone in North Carolina. Some had come to terms that there was no exit from the misfortune that lay ahead, whereas others held their heads high to work things out. It was Sunday morning, and just like regular times, everyone was expected to attend the morning service in the Church. Pastor Brent spent the night in the Church praying for the people of North Carolina, and the government to be of aid, and lastly for himself, so he could be able to find someone who was convincing enough to ease the doubting minds of the people. Pastor Brent was dark, a man of average height, he had a head full of dark brown hair and he also had big green eyes.

He walked towards the main auditorium of the Parkwood church holding his bible, sermon notes, and cordless microphone. It was already time for the service, but to his shock, he saw only five members of the congregation seated. With that look of awe, he looked around for his assistant, Pastor Mike, who was making his way towards him with brisk steps.

"Hello, Pastor Mike," Pastor Brent greeted him.

Pastor Mike smiled as he stopped to greet him, "Good day, Pastor Brent." He was tall and slender and a bit dark-colored. He had jet-black hair and blue eyes and was someone that everyone in the church considered handsome.

"Where is everyone?" Pastor Brent said as he looked over at the church auditorium again.

"I have asked the same question, sir, service is about to start and a lot of people, who serve as our regular congregation are still not here yet," Pastor Mike said as he shook his head and let out a soft sigh in disbelief.

"I cannot believe this," Pastor Brent said as he moved his hand from his forehead and placed it on his waist, he was already starting to get frustrated.

"Not to worry Pastor…," Pastor Mike said, "I have instructed some workers present here to find out what is going on."

Pastor Brent interrupted him suddenly, "We cannot start service without at least twenty people in attendance. What do we do for now, while we wait for more people to join us?" he said as he locked eyes with Pastor Mike.

"I could inform Minister Sam," he said pointing to a man sitting on one of the pews in the church auditorium, he was red-haired, light-skinned, and averagely tall. "I could tell him to lead worship for a few minutes if that is okay with," he said.

When minister Sam saw them, he hurried to join them. "Good morning, Pastors," he said as he looked at his watch to check the time.

"Good day," Pastor Brent and Pastor Mike both responded to his greetings.

Pastor Mike cleared his throat as began to speak, "So, you can see that not many people are here for service which is very odd, we are already on top of the issue, but we won't be able to start service without a substantial amount of people…so while we wait, can you lead us in a short worship session?" He said as he gave Minister Sam a light pat on his back.

Minister nodded as he moved to respond with a big smile, "Of course, I will."

"Great," Pastor Mike said as he smiled briefly at Minister Sam as he walked over to the altar.

"Shall we all rise?" Minister Sam said as he climbed the altar and waited for the few people in the congregation to stand.

While Minister Sam led worship, Pastor Brent called Pastor Mike into his church office for a brief meeting.

"Any word on what is going on yet?" Pastor Brent said as he ushered Pastor Mike into his office.

"Actually, I was just able to speak to Mr. Byrne's, the head of the church's follow-up team a few minutes ago," he said, "so many members expressed their concern. They are very scared about coming to church, and more scared about everything that seems to be happening recently," he said. "They prefer to stay in their homes, as they feel that staying in their homes is the only promised way of safety," Pastor Mike said as he tapped the office table lightly.

"Well, that is not very logical", Pastor Brent said as he looked over at Pastor Mike, "if anything, it is during times such as this one, that the church is expected to be a united front", he said as he wiped beads of sweat from his forehead, "looking at the number of people that turned up for service this morning, I was discouraged".

"You need not to worry Pastor," Pastor Mike said in an encouraging tone, "the Lord is with us."

"I guess we just have to go on with service, I don't think we can wait any longer, please notify Minister Sam so he can stop the worship session," Pastor Brent said as he started packing up the Bible and sermon notes along with his iPad and microphone.

"Alright…I will do just that," Pastor Mike said as he turned around and walked out of the church office.

Pastor Brent made his way to the altar towards the worshiping session, "thank you son," he whispered into Minister Sam's ears. Minister Sam nodded as he responded, "My pleasure."

"I first want to start by thanking you all…for making it to church on this blessed and beautiful Sunday morning, and I also want to say that my heart goes out to each and every one of you. The times that we are currently in are very unprecedented, and the situation we find ourselves in at the moment is somewhat confusing, but we will be victorious in the end. Can I say, is someone here in this auditorium today?" He thundered as he moved around the altar.

"Yes!!!!" the members responded with a loud shout.

"Can I get an amen?" Pastor Brent responded.

The congregation stood in unity as they responded to him, "Amen!"

"Take your seats in his wonderful presence," Pastor Brent said as he watched the members in the auditorium go back to their respective seats.

"Today, I want to talk something that is important in our lives, today we will discuss about trust…," he continued as he navigated through his iPad.

Laura had decided to tune in for the service that day after she managed to take a long bath after waking up earlier that morning. She loved waking up before the rest of the family so she could get things done before attending to her family.

She browsed through the television channels and saw that almost all the channels had now been disconnected, all except the one that broadcast Parkwood Church's services from time to time. She reached for the TV remote to increase the volume as Pastor Brent's voice filled up the living room.

"So today, as I said earlier, I am going to be talking to all of us about trust," Pastor spoke.

Laura noticed only a few members attended church that morning, she was not surprised given the current circumstances that they were all going through in North Carolina. She assumed that everyone would have preferred to remain in their homes for the sake of safety since no one understood what was going on, it seemed to be a situation that no one had a proper explanation for.

She focused on the TV screens once more as she watched Pastor Brent preach his sermon.

"What does trust mean? Or how do you know you trust someone?" He stopped for a second and then continued, "Trust has a lot to do with reliability, you know. You can say that you trust someone when you can rely on them," he cleared his throat as he continued, "Now, I would say this message is very timely, given the times that we are currently in."

"What does it mean to trust God?" Pastor Brent asked as he looked down at his bible and then looked up again, "Trusting in God means that you as a person are relying on God completely to take care of all your needs and all your burdens."

Just then, Kirk walked into the living room half asleep and slowly walked to Laura's side, "What is going on here?" He asked while rubbing his eyes with his left hand.

"Just thought I tune in and watch the service's live stream," Laura said as she lightly patted the chair smiling suggesting Kirk to come and sit beside her, "you want to come over here?"

"I don't know why you are still watching and listening to any of these guys," he said as he gave her a light kiss on her forehead, "how was your night?" He said, trying to get her attention.

Laura gently rolled her eyes as she looked up at him.

"What?" Kirk looked back at Laura trying not to laugh or get carried away by her expression.

"It's just one sermon…one message Kirk," she said as she stretched her arms up in frustration.

"What are they telling you now?" He asked moving his head side to side, trying to make Laura laugh, "what? Saying God's got you, fear not blah blah blah," he said as he burst out laughing in return.

"I'm serious Kirk, none of this is funny, none of anything going on around here is funny," she said as she responded with raised eyebrows.

"I am sorry. I just do not believe in any of this, none of what he is saying makes any sense to me. I have been trying to keep up and just support you all this while but, this is more than enough proof that your God or whoever does not exist. I do not think it should even be contested at all, it's all very clear now, there is no God, it's so simple, stop allowing yourself to be constantly controlled by these so-called fraudsters posing as Men of God," he said as he walked towards a chair in the living room.

"Wow…Kirk, I cannot believe you right now…," Laura said as she shook her head to express her disbelief, "you know what! It is just too early to start an argument, I do not have the strength to spoil for a fight," she said trying to stand up from the couch but struggled to do so.

"I'm not trying to argue with you babe, I am only just trying to be logical, it's pretty obvious now, all I'm saying is…let us all stop living in denial," Kirk said as he shrugged his shoulders.

Laura retaliated by reaching for a throw pillow on the couch that she was sitting on to throw at Kirk, "Ouch, which hurts," Kirk said as the pillow hit him, she chuckled as she stuck her tongue out, "That serves you right, you are just so annoying."

"Fine, I'll just leave before I get my head bitten off," Kirk said as he stood up from the couch and left the living room.

Laura turned to face the television stand and continued watching the live sermon that was on before her husband came to the living room.

"So trusting God has to do with loving him and depending on him wholeheartedly. Trusting God is something that as children of God, something that we as believers need to become very deliberate about in our walk with God and in our journey through life, it is not something that we can afford to be indifferent about. It is something that we must do, it is something that God who is our father truly requires of us," Pastor Brent said as he started turning the pages of his bible.

"Hmmm, that makes a lot of sense," Laura said as she nodded in agreement with what Pastor Brent had just said.

"Turn your bibles with me to Proverbs 3 verses 5-6", Pastor Brent said as he stopped to clear his throat, "can you all do me a favor, we are all going to read it aloud together okay? If you are there shout hallelujah."

Pastor Brent said as he stopped to look around at the congregation, "If you are there…shout hallelujah," he said as he looked around waiting for their response.

Then two of the members of the congregation stood up as they shouted in unison, "Hallelujah!"

Pastor Brent smiled broadly as he looked down at his bible and said, "It is good to know that you all are still with me", he stopped to clear his throat as he looked up at them again, "Ok, we are all going to read this passage together", he said as he gestured to the members of the congregation to start reading the bible passage.

"Trust in the Lord with all your heart and do not depend on your own understanding, seek his will in all you do and he shall direct your path", Pastor Brent looked up from his bible as he removed his glasses and stepped down from the altar and he started walking around the first row and pew of the church, "Now, just like everything I have been sharing with us and telling us about what it means to trust God, this passage of the bible further puts an emphasis on what it means to trust God and why it is so important.

Laura moved around uncomfortably on the couch and propped herself with a pillow to adjust her sitting position. She watched Pastor

Brent as he continued to preach, "You see as believers, we will go through different trials and temptations that would sometimes demand all of us, our emotions, our time, our resources, and any other possible thing we can ever think of but truly, we can only get through those very tough situations by looking unto one sole source, by looking unto the source of life itself…which is none other than God…"

James and Miranda walked into the living room and ran over to Laura's side to give her a long and tight hug with their Dad, Kirk following them. "Hi, Mommy," James said as he giggled loudly after they stopped hugging. Laura pulled James into another hug and gave him a kiss on his forehead, "how are you, my baby? How was your night? Did you sleep well?" She said as she held him waiting for him to respond.

"I did not sleep well mama…when will all of this be over," James said as he rubbed his eyes with the back of his hands.

"oh baby…", Laura said as she rubbed his cheek lightly and smiled at him, "I also have no idea why these things are happening and why they are happening in the first place, I just know…I have a feeling that everything will blow over soon, so do not worry, okay?" She said looking at him and Miranda, "Hi Miranda, how are you? How was your night? Did you sleep well?"

Miranda winced to express her displeasure, this meant that she also did not sleep well the night before, and everything that had been happening made her extremely restless. She barely had two straight hours of sleep the night before and was also very worried about Mike, her elder brother who had left for college earlier that year. "I also was not able to sleep very well, I have just been extremely restless…and worried, I have not been able to get through to Mike, he has not responded to my last text messages and none of the emails that I sent him recently have gone through. Has anyone spoken to him or heard from him?" She asked as she settled down on the couch beside her mother.

Kirk and Laura looked at each other, Laura had also tried to reach out to him a few times since the announcement was made on the news and she also had not gotten any significant replies from him. Kirk brought his phone out of his pocket and looked at it, "I got a text message from him this morning…," Laura sighed as her hands went to her chest. Kirk looked at his phone again and started reading, *"Hi, Dad…I know that by now, you all must have been so worried about me, I am so sorry. I am also sorry for not responding to your text messages or emails, I was just very overwhelmed…so, the school management announced that they will be evacuating and sending all students home from school for the sake of safety. I will be leaving school today with the school stipulated transport scheme and hopefully, I should join you back at home later today or early tomorrow morning, my love to Mom, Miranda, and James,"* and then Kirk put his phone back in his pocket.

"Thank goodness he is okay…I have been so worried," Laura said as she looked up at Kirk then at Miranda whose mood instantly became better after her dad read the text message to them, she was incredibly happy that at the very least, her brother was safe.

The Wednesday after, Pastor Brent announced an important bible study session where they were going to discuss as a group, some bible passages centered on the topic that he had talked about the previous Sunday during service. He arranged them into groups and told them to discuss the passages, he stayed worried all week as he was very displeased with how the church seemed to be sidelined by some of its members due to the ongoing conflict. He was also starting to question God's love and presence, he felt as if God had forgotten them.

The first group had Minister Sam as their leader and they spoke about different passages, a member of the group who was a youth member said one of the passages reminded him about trust in God which was found in 1ˢᵗ Peter 5;7; "cast all your anxiety on him because he cares for you". Another member referenced a passage in 1ˢᵗ Thessalonians 5;16-18; "give thanks in all circumstances for this is God's will for you in Christ

Jesus", a female member of the group referenced Psalm 34;17; "when the righteous cry for help, the lord hears and delivers them from all their troubles".

Two other members quoted two other verses of scripture and passages in the Bible, Romans 8:28; "and we know that all things work together for good for those that love him and are called according to his purpose", and the other quoted Isaiah 40:31; "those who wait upon the lord shall renew their strength, they shall mount up with wings as eagles, they shall run and not be weary they shall walk and not faint".

Chapter Four

S ince the announcement was made about an asteroid hitting the earth, everyone in North Carolina had been holed up in their houses because there was also no announcement that predicted when that would be happening apart from the few unexpected changes that had happened with them over the last few weeks. They were now extremely low on food and home supplies as these were only available for purchase in a few stores in the outer parts of North Carolina and many people were afraid of taking trips outside their homes. Some people did have metallic chips planted in the middle of their heads and wrists, so many events that had happened were now becoming questionable. What Lance saw in his dream had turned into a reality. Some people decided to try the chip to see how it works because they were afraid of not being able to get their money out of the bank. The government was offering incentives for the first hundred people in each state to try it out. Everyone seemed to be living in a nightmare of their own, and Laura thought it might be What was mention in the bible that the chip was a source of their income and living, "so that they could not buy or sell unless they had the mark, which is the name of the beast or the number of its name."

Revelation 13:17 NIV

Earlier that day, the mayor released a widely spread broadcast through the only functioning means of communication; the megaphones, "I must greet every member of each community in North Carolina. I am very aware now that the times that we are in are unprecedented and difficult to understand. I also want to applaud you all for your strength and courage, for standing together in one accord as a united front during the occurrence of these strange events. It is very admirable, although we may not understand why these things are happening, I want us to understand that every single thing that has a beginning also has an end, and on that note, I want to remind us all yet again just in case we may have forgotten, this will all end soon…"

"This, like every other time in life, is only a season and I am very hopeful that all of these will come to an end soon. I want to state that while this happens, we should all endeavor to do everything that we can to maintain stability within our state. We cannot afford to be reckless in any form or leave anything to chance; I want to say, let us all be watchful, and we must be very deliberate about our security in our homes, communities, and the state at large. Considering the current situation, the entire state of North Carolina will be put under compulsory and statewide security starting today. So, I want to implore each of us to take everything I say seriously, as this is the major way, I know that we will all be able to get through this phase."

"We should all be very vigilant and constantly always maintain the security of our individual homes and at the very least. Let us also be deliberate about being conscious of our surroundings and our environment from time to time as we move ahead in this exceedingly difficult journey. Let us as a people, bring our beloved state out of this situation successfully through whatever capacity we have, we will try to employ the assistance of all the relevant teams that pertain to this particular situation as time goes on and as time permits, and I am also very certain that we would get through all of this together", he said as he ended his speech and the megaphones went off.

Later that day, Laura planned to hold a feast for the family, she asked Miranda to join her in the kitchen for lunch preparations while Kirk and her son took a nap in their bedroom. She was occupied with preparing the stuffing while Miranda made the stir fry vegetables when she heard the TV suddenly come on, "This is an emergency broadcast from FSN news network, I am Lori Sage reporting live from my home office with a new report about the expected asteroid…”

Laura's heart dropped when she heard the last statement the reporter made, and out of shock she almost dropped the pan from her hand. Miranda rushed over to her side to quickly collect the pan of stuffing from her mom and she went over to put it on the kitchen table. Laura seemed like she had seen a ghost. Miranda patted her lightly on her shoulder and gave her a slight rub on her back as she led her back to the living room so they could watch the live broadcast.

They both settled in the living room as the news reporter continued the broadcast, “As we all were informed that an asteroid, precisely a meteor, is expected to be coming down to earth…FSN News Network has the latest information for its viewers. According to the research team of scientists in North Carolina, the asteroid is expected to reach by tonight or in the early hours of tomorrow morning …”

Laura cupped her mouth with her hands as she let out a very loud gasp and looked over to Miranda who was sitting directly beside her, “oh my gosh…Miranda, your brother is not back from school yet, what is going on?” Miranda tried to calm her down as she patted her back again, “Mom, try not to worry, okay? Mike is already on his way, you heard Dad reading out his text earlier. I am sure he is almost here anyway, try not to worry please, it is not good for you…”

The reporter's voice came up again just as Miranda was about to give her mother a light head rub to relax her, “I want to state that it is important that we all begin adequate preparations especially for the period this asteroid will be landing on earth and admonish us also, to make appropriate preparations for our overall wellbeing and security while we experience this never-seen-before event. We have been informed of the precise landing of this event so all that we must do at this moment is prepare…All Right then, until I come your way next time, I am Lori Sage reporting for FSN News, thank you,” then the TV went off again.

She went over to the kitchen to set the table for Lunch and then went where her dad and brother had been sleeping. She tapped her dad lightly on his shoulder, "Hi Dad, it's time for lunch please come over to eat."

Kirk turned over to look at her and rubbed his face, "Ok," he said and carried James from the bed, and followed her out of the room.

Laura had been extremely startled following the news of the confirmation of the asteroid possibly coming to Earth that day or the day after and she was particularly worried about her son who had reached out earlier in the day, telling them that he was already on his way back from his college, but it had been hours after that, and they still had not heard from him yet. "Mom…," she had been lost in thought and barely realized that Miranda had been trying to get her attention.

"Mom…look", Miranda raised her eyebrows in the direction of the serving plates that they placed on the dining table, Laura had a spoonful of stuffing that she was about to serve on her husband's plate, but accidentally spilled on the table, "Oh my God…I am so sorry", she said, "Miranda, could you get some napkins from the kitchen please?"

"Alright, Mom," Miranda said as she walked to the kitchen.

Just then, they heard a knock on the front door, ever since the news broke out, they had not received any visitors in their homes aside from their neighbor and Laura's closest friend, "who is there?" Kirk yelled out from his seat; they kept hearing the knock on the door, so he went over to check. On opening the door, his eyes lit up, "Hey buddy," Kirk said as Mike replied, "Hi Dad," and quickly pulled him into a hug.

Laura and Miranda heard Mike's voice from inside the kitchen and rushed to the living room. Miranda ran over to Mike, "I have missed you! I missed you so much," she said as Mike hugged her and let out a soft chuckle, "Hi baby sis, I missed you too, how are you?" Mirada smiled as she looked at him, "I'm trying to fake it and say I'm good given the current circumstance…but I am just so happy that you are here, I am happy that you are back home."

"I am so…happy to be back home too. I missed all of you…," Mike's eyes lit up again as his mom approached him.

"My baby boy…I have missed you so much. I was so scared and worried about you," Laura said as she cupped her hands with her mouth and tears started falling from her eyes.

"aww, mom…please don't cry," Mike said as he embraced Laura. "I missed you so much," he said as he gave her a soft peck on her forehead.

Laura lightly rubbed the small of Mike's back as she replied, "I'm just happy you are safe, we just made lunch…do you want a plate?" she asked as she looked up at him.

" Of course, I do," Mike said as he made his way into the kitchen to serve a plate for himself, "what are we having?" He said as he opened the serving dishes, "Wow, just what I was craving."

Everyone across the table burst into laughter. Laura was simply happy that her family was now reunited.

Later that day, the expected asteroid eventually landed on Earth, and for the first time in a while, this was something that brought everyone out of their homes. Everyone wanted to see the descending of the asteroid even though it was not advisable safety-wise. The very awaited sight of the asteroid pulled together people from every nook and corner, but rather than excitement, it left them in a state of despair.

Chapter Five

Miranda was happy that her brother had returned home, and she was particularly very hopeful that the clouds hanging over their heads at this period were going to disappear soon enough and that they could go back to their normal lives or at the very least, go back to life as they knew it could be. She also had been extremely worried about her mom who had been very distant from her family and had also been very jittery lately.

Miranda spent most of her time studying in the morning, hoping to get back to school at the earliest. She still had not told anyone about her failed tests and her struggles with school work, not even Mike who was also her closest pal and confidant, she always loved talking to him about anything that she had a problem with, but this time, she figured it was only right that she kept this to herself, she did not want to add to their current problems which she knew affected all of them individually and as family one way or the other.

She was having a challenging time trying to understand her studies when she heard a loud beep on her phone. She closed her English textbook and squinted at her phone screen to check the notification. It was a message from her friend at school, Alyssa, "Hi Miranda, I was just checking on you, I hope you are good, how are you holding up? How is your Mom doing? How is James? I hope your brother Mike is back from school now. I just cannot believe that all of this is happening, it just feels so unreal, and it is so shocking that this is what our life is like at the moment, can you believe it? I mean…who would have thought that this would ever happen…" She stopped for a few minutes before continuing to read the rest of her text.

"Anyway, I just hope everything ends real soon because I am not doing too well, I miss everyone at school, I miss being able to go outside and being able to just walk or take my usual jogs in the morning before school. I miss being able to go to the grocery store, I miss being able to walk down to Central Park on Saturdays with my mom and sister. I just miss what life was like before all of this started happening, I am gradually starting to lose it… I miss you so much, but I am looking forward to the silver lining in all of this and I hope I see you soon. I am going to give you the biggest hug possible when I eventually see you and I just hope that you are holding up and doing well at the very least… if it feels like we're slowly losing everything, we should not add losing our minds to it, please I know it is difficult, but try to stay sane…I love you".

Miranda smiled brightly and let out a huge sigh after reading it. She missed Alyssa, and this text message from her had to be very prompt because she was so tired already of everything that had been happening to them. She tapped on her phone screen to reply but before even she could begin typing a beam of joy consumed her as midst of all the chaos, she still had a loving friend like Alyssa.

"My dearest Alyssa…," she paused and smiled before writing any further, "I must say that your text message comes at a time where it is really needed, your message is a very timely one. I want to say thank you so much for checking up on me, it means a lot to me. I am so happy that I got your message, you have literally no idea how it makes me feel, it is no wonder why they say, people who love each other the most…though separated by distance, are always joined together by their hearts, in a time such as this. I am grateful for our friendship and everything that it has brought my way, truly our friendship has brought me so much comfort…"

"I must say I am so thankful for you, my friend; you have been consistent in my life through all the years, and while we are still here… I just want to say I appreciate you so much, thank you for everything that you are and mean to me, I am so happy that we are still here together.

My mom is out of touch lately, and I completely understand it, given the challenges we have been going through. I am so worried about her, she is pregnant and vulnerable now, and I don't want anything to happen to her, my dad is okay…at least he seems to be."

Miranda paused again as she looked up at the ceiling of her room, she had started tearing up, which was not something that she was used to, she hated crying or being made to look vulnerable at any point in time. She dabbed at the corners of her eyes to clean up her tears before she looked down at her phone again to continue texting, "I am so happy that Mike came back home just in time. I would have been sadder than I already am if I found out that anything had happened to him…and he needs a haircut as soon as possible…," she stopped to laugh loudly as she dabbed the corner of her right eye to stop another tear from falling from it.

"We have not had the time to talk…just us two alone, about everything happening in school, everything happening with us, we do have a lot to catch up on. want to talk to him about school since it is what I am struggling with now because knowing my brother, he always seems to have a solution for everything…well, everything except what is happening at the moment, he seems happy though…more so than usual. I guess he has just been his typical bubbly self, always positive and smiling, and always looking at the brighter side of things. I must say this is one of the many reasons why I love him. My brother is the best big brother in the entire universe and world put together."

"And lastly…James, James is a handful, if you must know…he is in the super active stage now and he is running around like crazy, he is turning the whole house upside down and it is becoming super hard to run after him. I have to stop to catch my breath…", she said as she stopped to laugh again, she looked around her room as she continued typing on her phone, "he has grown so much since the last time that you saw him", he says the words, "I'm done", every time he goes to use the bathroom or when he is done eating and wants us to help him clear his plate, at this point, he is going to eat everything in the house and run us out of all our supplies, and that is going to be a tough situation to be in because there is literally nowhere for us to get any more supplies, we can't even get out of the house!"

"At this point, I am sure you are wondering how I am doing since I have practically talked about every other person but myself…well, I have to say…I am also not doing very well. I just pretend to be okay, but deep down, I am extremely devastated. I have no idea why this is happening, and I do not plan to find out why, it seems like God has abandoned us. It feels like the world is coming to an end and if it is the latter, it makes me scared about what is to come because I am not dealing so well with everything that is happening and I just want all of this to be over as soon as possible."

"I miss you so much my friend, I wish that I could come over to your house and just give you the biggest bear hug because I need one. It's so crazy how one minute, you are in school thinking of how to survive it and all that comes with it, including your struggle with not being able to keep up with school work, and the next minute you are holed up in your house without knowing when next you will be able to get out and smell the flowers on your front porch again or just be able to go out of your house for a much needed refreshing walk to the park…"

"It is crazy that we have not been able to see or go about our normal lives and daily routines that we are already used to in the last couple of weeks and it is coming to me as a surprise, how quickly life can change for someone or a group of people in the snap of a finger. I miss my normal life and I want to be able to get back to it. I cannot believe that I am saying this…as much as I hate being in school, I cannot wait to get back to school. I hope that we can continue talking like this, it is one of the ways that I can manage to be a bit sane. I love you too, I love you very much my heart could burst into pieces…it is at times like this that I am reminded of what Michaelers, and I cannot wait to see you soon, I love you."

She smiled as she placed her phone on her bedside table, and she moved to pick up her English textbook to continue her attempt at trying to solve some problems and hopefully understand them. Just then, she heard a knock on her door, and she got up from her bed to go and check to see who it was. It was her dad, he smiled brightly at her as she opened the door, "Hi girl… we need to talk…come join all of us in the living room, okay?" Miranda smiled shortly at him and replied, "I am going to join you soon," her dad nodded as he responded, "Alright, we are all waiting for you," as he left her room to go back to the living room.

Miranda walked into the living room to see the rest of her family waiting for her, she went over to sit beside Mike and as she sat down, she was quick to speak, "what is going on?" she said as she looked around at all of them. Her dad let out a sigh as she clasped his hands together and moved to respond to her. "Well, I just wanted us to sit down together… and talk about everything that is going on…it has been a while since we have all been together like this under one roof. I am happy that Mike is back home with us now safe and sound…"———————————————

"I just wanted to check in with everyone to see how we are all doing. I am sure that we have a lot of questions about a lot of things, particularly about everything that has been going on with us…" he stopped to release his hands and let out another sigh of relief, "I am going to start with you Mike…how are you doing?" Mike smiled as he looked at all of them and then looked back at his dad Kirk, "Thank you so much for doing this Dad, it means a lot to me…" He stopped to look at Miranda who smiled brightly at him before he continued speaking, "I just want to start by saying that I am happy to be reunited with my family again. I missed all of you, and all the while, I just kept praying to come home from school, unharmed and in one piece, and I am happy that it happened that way…"

Kirk interrupted him before he could be able to continue speaking, "So…how was school? What was happening down there, huh? We all missed you and were so worried about you when the news first came out…" he said as he gave Mike a pat on his back Mike laughed nervously as he responded to his dad, "I did not get to hear much about the news at first. There were rumors going around in school, but the management and authorities did not speak about it or confirm it. All I could remember was…this sudden announcement from the school's dean of academic affairs about an immediate evacuation."

"At first, I was shocked about it because I did not think that it was anything serious. I did not even think that it was THIS serious at all," he said as he gestured with his hands and smiled, "I just want to say, in as much as we all do not understand anything that is going on now. I am hopeful that everything will come to an end soon and everything that is happening will soon come to an end. I am looking forward to the time when our lives will go back to normal again, and I am also hoping that it is very soon."

Kirk smiled as he looked over at Laura who was busy scolding James for trying to jump over the couch yet again. Miranda looked over to her mom and younger brother and she at once burst out laughing, she was right about one thing. She was right about James being a handful. Laura screamed as she tried to make James sit on the couch properly, "James, sit down right now," she said as she pointed her finger at him and looked at him with a very firm and stern look on her face, James crouched and sat back down on the couch while trying to hold back tears.

Laura looked over at Kirk and smiled brightly at him, "This boy is really a lot, I am so tired of screaming at him. He just cannot stay put and I am at my wit's end right now. I cannot deal with him; can you handle it?" She said as she looked over at Kirk with her eyebrows raised. Kirk smirked his lips and looked over at James and he cleared his throat, "Now boy…you know very well that you should not be climbing the couch… that is bad, okay? Are you a bad boy?" Kirk asked as he looked at James while raising his eyebrows at him.

James shook his head as he looked at his dad. Kirk smiled shortly as he looked at him, "Very good…now what do you say to your mom?" James turned around to face Laura and he said, "I am sorry, mommy," Laura pulled him into a hug and pecked him on his forehead, "That's my baby boy! Now do not do that again, okay?" James chuckled loudly as he hugged her back and responded to her, "I won't do what will make you sad again, Mommy," Laura smiled so much her eyes started to tear up and she started turning red on her face, "You are so cute!" she said as she squealed loudly.

Kirk let out a soft sigh and he turned to face all of them again, "Now let us move on to you, Miranda, it's your turn, how have you been holding up?" He said as he waited for her to respond. Miranda adjusted herself on the couch, "Ummmm…", she hesitated but continued to speak, "I am trying to stay sane…, like Mike said, I'm just happy that we are all together, and it's been rough, and crazy for us these past few weeks, but I know that as long as we are together. There is nothing that we cannot get through. I know that one day we are going to get through this. It may not look like it now, but we have each other and that is all that Michaelers to me at this very moment," she said as she smiled and reached out for her mother's hand. Laura turned to her as she smiled and stroked the back of her hand.

Mike smiled as he pulled his mom and Miranda into a hug and he carefully stroked their hair, "I am so happy to be with all of you right now," he said as he placed kisses on their forehead, respectively. Kirk was determined to ask every one of his family members about their health and well-being. He had been bothered about all of them since all the weird things had started happening. His fear grew stronger when the meteor hit the earth and forced them to remain indoors, he just wished that his family were extremely safe at this time, and he was ready to do anything to ensure their happiness and safety even though it looked bleak at the moment.

"Before I go on…Miranda, is there anything you would like to share with us? Anything that you may be having issues with anything at all?" He paused and looked at her. Miranda felt her heart skip within her as it began racing, "*What does he mean by that? Did the school reach out to him, what does he mean by his sudden question, maybe the school reached out to him…I am not ready for any of that just yet, I am not ready to tell them anything about school yet, not with everything going on…*", she trailed off while thinking and became lost in her thoughts.

"Miranda…," she heard someone calling her name but could not figure out who it was, "Miranda…," she looked up and saw that her dad was calling her, "Yes…Dad," she said as she winced shortly before looking at him properly. "Do you have anything that you want to share with us? Do you have any issues?" she stopped and smiled nervously, "No Dad, I do not have any issues. I am fine Dad, there is no need to worry about me."

Kirk capped his hands and raised his brows as he said, "Alright then if you say so…I'm happy you are okay."

Laura had been extremely worried about her family and worried for their safety, she had also not heard from Lance and his wife Marie in the last week, which was also very unusual as they always checked in on each other from time to time. She was praying and hoping that they were both safe and she hoped that they would all be able to see each other when it was safe for them to do so. She decided that she was going to reach out to them before the end of the day, she thought to bring it up while she was with her family, "Kirk…have you heard anything from Lance or Marie. I have been worried about them." Kirk shook his head as he responded, "That's true…no, I haven't heard from them…" This made Laura more anxious, "OH, I am hoping that they are fine though. I am just going to pray for them…"

Kirk snapped as soon as he heard her and he instantly cut her off before she could finish her statement, "There you go again with this whole prayer and God talk," he said as he gestured, raising his hands in frustration.

"What do you mean by…here I go again, Kirk?" Laura retaliated with a sharp and raised tone in her voice.

"Aren't you tired of all that already? What kind of 'so-called God,' sits back and watches ALL of this happen?" Kirk said as he moved his hands in a circular motion.

Mike stopped him and tried calming him down, "Hey Dad, come on, it's okay."

"What do you mean by it is okay? Do me a favor…talk to your mom, none of this makes sense. I am just about tired of her always going on about this God that obviously does not exist…"

Laura's eyes welled up with tears and she was already starting to turn red, she always turned red, and her complexion always changed anytime she got angry, "You know what?" Miranda tried to stop her from speaking and she stood up to try to pacify her by stroking her shoulder. Laura was too angry at this point to notice Miranda, and she continued speaking anyway. "I have had it with your annoying remarks and disrespect these last few weeks, fine! You can sit there and go on about how you do not believe God exists, that is all on you, but you are not going to turn my kids' minds away from him, I won't let you do that!" she said as she raised her eyebrows while sternly looking at him.

"You can say whatever you want…but what I'm saying is very true and obvious, I just want you to stop the pretense okay? it is getting old," Kirk responded sharply.

Laura squealed as her hands folded and her fists formed, "I cannot even look at you right now, you are so unbelievable, Kirk!" She said as she struggled to stand up from the couch and then she looked at her children who had all gone quiet, she stomped her feet as she walked out of the living room.

After the fight between Laura and Kirk, Mike stayed in the living room till evening without going back to his room. He grabbed a small pack of popcorn from the Kitchen and wanted to watch a movie. While Miranda went back to her room to continue studying before dinner time, Mike decided to watch one of his favorite TV shows, "freedom" as it had been a while since he last watched it. He tuned in the channel and adjusted himself on the couch, it was almost time for the show to start.

Just then, the news came on, Mike was shocked and called out for everyone to come to the living room, "Guys! The news just came on," he said as he dropped the pack of popcorn on the side stool. Miranda came running to the living room followed by Kirk who placed James on his shoulders as he walked briskly to the living room to watch the news. Laura came in shortly after with her hands placed on her baby bump and they all sat down while waiting for the news to come on fully.

"Hi there, I am Lori Sage reporting live for the FSN news network from my home office bringing yet another emergency news broadcast your way. I have a colleague and special guest with me who is also tuned in and will be joining me for the live broadcast this evening, this is John Burke…," she paused for a few minutes so the other reporter could join in the broadcast.

"Alright good evening, everyone, I am Lori Sage, and with me is…," she stopped as she waited for the other reporter to respond.

"John Burke," the other reporter said as he smiled briefly.

"Alright…let us get into the headlines for today…it is reported that the meteor asteroid came down to earth as we all are aware of now and unfortunately, we have to report that this asteroid has posed a lot of ripple effects…," Lori paused as she waited for John to continue.

"North Carolina's most renowned scientists have formulated a group to study the impact of asteroid ever since its landing, and a word has gotten out that is brought many ripple and crippling effects with it … and starting now, we must collectively embrace ourselves to face these effects. There is a higher chance that North Carolina along with its neighboring communities might start experiencing calamities such as tsunamis and earthquakes …"

Laura looked over at Kirk as they both let out a loud gasp and then she looked over at Mike and Miranda who were extremely dumbfounded. The air was then filled with silence until Miranda spoke, "I cannot believe this, when is all this going to end?" there was a loud squeak in her voice.

"I know right, so now we are just supposed to wrap our heads around the possibilities of tsunamis and what…earthquakes possibly sweeping all of us up, like what is all this?" Mike said as he let out a sigh expressing his disbelief and frustration.

"I know it's hard…and what I am saying might possibly not make any sense to all of you, but please, I want all of us to try and remain calm," Kirk said as he tried to pacify all of them.

Laura shrieked as she looked at him, she was still upset with him about the argument that they had earlier and he still had not tried to apologize to her, "yeah right," she said under her breath as she looked away.

Kirk rolled his eyes as he looked at her. He did not have any energy within him to pick a fight with her, that was the last thing that they needed in the face of everything going on and with everything else that was bound to happen with and to them going forward. "Alright, fine! I am sorry, okay?" He said as he turned over to her. His eyes showed how sorry he truly was.

Laura was not pleased, and she continued to look away and she folded her arms together as she did that, "I am so not buying that apology," she said as she rested her back on the couch.

"I just said I was sorry," Kirk said as he clenched his hands together.

Miranda looked over at her mom and she went over to her side, "Mom, Dad is sorry okay, he did not mean for any of this to happen. The last thing that we all need right now, in this moment, is you guys fighting or even being at each other's throats please", she said as she stroked her mother's back lightly trying to console her.

"It is fine, it's alright. Fighting is very useless anyway, it is not something I want to spend my supposed last days before we are all swept up by any of these things that they claim are coming our way," Laura said as she let out a huge sigh. Kirk came over to her side and pulled her into a hug as she looked up at him and smiled while he planted a small kiss on her forehead and smiled back at her.

They stood up and left the living room to retire to bed followed by their children, Mike, Miranda, and James.

The next morning, Laura's sound sleep was disturbed by some vibrating effect. She opened her eyes and saw Kirk sleeping peacefully beside her. She adjusted her pillows against the bed headboards and sat up straight, just then she again felt waves of vibrations as if they came from the earth itself. This frightened her even more, so she turned to Kirk and tried waking him up.

"Kirk…wake up," she said as she hurriedly shook him trying to wake him up.

"What is it?" Kirk said sleepily without turning to look at her.

"Can't you feel anything?" Laura asked as she tried to wake him up again.

"Feel what?" Kirk asked, "I can't feel anything."

Just then, the vibrations kicked in again and Kirk sat up straight. "What is that?" He asked while looking at her.

"I don't know Kirk, I felt them while I was still trying to get some sleep and that was when I tried to wake you up," Laura said as she looked at him and started panicking.

Kirk stood up from the bed and he almost lost his balance as he stood up.

"Oh my God!" Laura said as she looked at him, "Please be careful."

Just then, the megaphones came on, "This is the state head of security, Barry Jameses, word has just gotten to us that Ohio is currently experiencing a serious earthquake and that is the reason why we are experiencing these uncommon ground vibrations. I want to appeal to all of us to seek all necessary safety measures while we try to maintain the security of the state on our end. Please if you notice anything odd, do not fail to raise the necessary alarm and make it known as soon as possible, we will get through this hopefully," the megaphones then went off.

Chapter Five (cont.)

Ever since the announcement about the earthquake in the neighboring states, Laura had been extremely worried. Even though she tried hard to remain calm, she was still not sure what new disaster might strike tomorrow. She was concerned about her family and friends' safety, it started to feel like her faith had started to wither.

She left her bed to prepare breakfast for her family. With Mike's return, it was going to be his first breakfast with family, so she decided to make blueberry pancakes and eggs. Miranda followed her into the kitchen to aid her with coffee and preparing oatmeal for James, as he always took oatmeal with pancakes instead of scrambled eggs. Miranda walked into the kitchen, put a pot of water on the stove, and reached for the big pack of oats in the kitchen cabinet.

"Oohh," Laura said as she placed her hands on her rounded belly, she had been feeling increased kicks and movement all morning ever since she got up from bed feeling uneasy and after she noticed all the vibrations.

Miranda looked at Laura as she went over to meet her where she was standing, "Hey mom…are you okay? Is everything alright?"

"Hehhh," Laura said as she dropped her hands from her belly, "this little one is really kicking my insides, your brother or sister sure is feisty," she said as she placed a round pan on the stove and poured the pancake mix into a plastic bowl. She reached for a whisk on the spoon stand, and she started to make the pancake dough.

Miranda laughed loudly as her hands went to her mouth, "I'm sure he or she is feeling all the emotions, they are probably feeding off the energy around which is totally normal," she said as she put on the coffee maker.

"I guess you are right babe…at least he or she is still moving, that way I know whoever is in here…", Laura said as she placed her hands on her rounded belly again, "with these kicks, I know that whoever is in here is alright, and that is all I need to know at this moment". Just then she was interrupted by Miranda's scream, "Mom!" Laura did not realize that she accidentally poured water all over the kitchen table as she spoke.

"Oh my God!" Laura exclaimed as she started snapping her fingers.

"What is it?" Miranda asked as she started panicking. The last thing that she needed at that moment was another nightmare, they already had a lot of things going on and she was definitely not ready to take on any further stress on her mind.

"I need a towel…please can you get me one of the kitchen towels quick," Laura said as she looked up at Miranda and then looked at the kitchen table again.

Miranda hurriedly went to the side of the kitchen where the towel was placed on an iron rack on the wall and she reached out to get one of them, "Here you go, Mom," she reached out to Laura as she hurriedly handed the kitchen towel to her.

"Thank you," Laura said as she took the kitchen towel from Miranda and began to slowly clean up the kitchen table.

Kirk walked in at that moment, his hands went up in the air showing his excitement, "I smell coffee," he said as he dashed into the kitchen with a big smile spread across his face, the smile almost turned to a frown as his eyes landed on the kitchen table.

"What happened here?" he gasped after he looked at the Kitchen table.

"Mom spilled some water while she was trying to make the pancakes earlier," Miranda replied as she looked over to her mom while she was standing at the other side of the kitchen table.

Kirk ran over to Laura's side and began to turn her around, "Oh my God! Are you okay? I hope you are not hurt. How is my baby?"

Laura laughed hysterically as she looked at Kirk, whenever he was in panic mode, it was a fun sight to behold, "such the drama queen…", she said as she burst into laughter again, "so many questions all at once…", she let out a big sigh and went on to place her hands on his shoulders in an attempt to calm him down, "It is just water okay?" she said as she looked into his eyes, "It's not a cause for alarm, there is no need to worry okay? I am perfectly fine."

Kirk let out a sigh as he placed his right hand on his forehead, "Are you sure you are fine? How is the baby?" he asked as he moved to examine Laura again.

Miranda laughed aloud as she noticed the expression on her dad's face, "Dad, she is fine," she said as she reached for the kitchen towel and continued to clean the kitchen table up.

"I'm fine, I promise you…if anything comes up, you will be the first to know, okay?" Laura said as she looked up at Kirk and went on to stroke his shoulders smoothly.

"Are you sure?" Kirk asked again as he looked at her.

"I am fine, okay?" Laura said as she looked at him and she rolled her eyes at him afterward.

She continued to make the pancake mix as she picked up the whisk and she gestured to Miranda to continue making the oatmeal for James.

After twenty minutes, Laura and Miranda started to set the dining table for breakfast.

"Breakfast is ready!" Laura called out as she placed the large platter of pancakes on the dining table, and she moved to settle on one of the chairs as she started plating James's food.

James came prancing to the dining table while holding his teddy bear, "Good morning mama," he said as he rubbed his eyes and went over to grab his mom's legs to hug her.

Laura bent over to pick him up and she pulled his cheeks, "How is my baby doing today?"

James chuckled as he looked into Laura's eyes, "Fine...I saw a dinosaur in my dream."

Laura let out a high gasp as she looked at him and went on to tickle him, "You saw a dinosaur?" she said as she tickled him some more.

"Yes," James said as he bent his head forward giggling loudly. Laura sat James on the floor as she squared her eyes with his, "Are you ready for breakfast?" she asked as she waited for him to respond.

James smiled as he looked at her and nodded while his eyes lit up brightly, "Yes mama!" he replied excitedly.

"Can you guess what we are having?" Laura asked as she smiled at him again.

James looked at her as he placed his teddy bear on the table, and she picked it up and placed it on a chair in the dining table area.

"Guess what we are having," Laura asked him again before looking up when she heard Kirk and Mike walk into the kitchen and dining area. She let out a huge sigh as she looked at them and shook her head, "Finally, you both have decided to grace us with your presence," she said sarcastically.

Mike started to laugh hysterically and almost began to choke on his laughter, Miranda quickly gave him a glass of water and then went over to serve James his plate of oatmeal.

"Thank you," James replied as Miranda placed his hot bowl of oatmeal in front of him.

"You are welcome," Miranda said, and she winced with a short smile as she responded.

James picked up his spoon and scooped a generous portion of oatmeal into his mouth.

Kirk burst out laughing as he was trying to serve his part of the pancakes and eggs that Laura made for breakfast. "My boy is so funny…," he said as he moved to the kitchen and dining area and placed his plate of food across James's seat, "He is such a comedian," he said as he looked over to Laura who started laughing out loud.

"He gets that side of him from you…you know?" Laura said as she looked at James and then looked back at Kirk. "You used to be extremely funny back in the day," Laura said as she winked at him.

"So, what…you mean I am not funny anymore?" Kirk asked as he looked at Laura, this time not hiding the look of extreme surprise from his face.

"I am not trying to fight with you babe…come on," Laura blurted out as she was starting to get irritated by Kirk's attitude.

"Mom… Dad, please do not fight," Mike said as he was serving his breakfast and as he gestured to his sister to serve him a cup of coffee.

Miranda went over to the coffee maker. She picked up a mug and started making Mike a cup of coffee as he asked.

"I know there are a lot of things going on with us and with everyone around us, I understand that…", Mike said as he moved to sit on one of the chairs in the dining area where everybody was, "Please…I just want to beg the two of you, please don't fight, this is the time for you both to be more united than ever. It is not the time to pick a fight over unnecessary things, we all just need to be each other's peace at this point in time," he said as he looked at his mother and then father.

"You are right son…," Kirk nodded as he grabbed his cup of coffee and took a huge sip from it, "I agree with you a hundred percent," he paused as he looked over to Laura who was tending to James after he spilled a big blurb of oatmeal on his shirt.

He stood up from the chair that he was sitting on and went over to her side and tried to get her to look at him, Laura was too angry to pretend that she was not starting to get ticked off by Kirk's recent change in attitude, she felt like it was starting to affect their relationship as a whole and to make Michaelers worse, their kids were starting to notice the shift.

"Look Kirk, I am tired of arguing with you. I have very little energy for that given our present circumstances. I don't want to fight anymore Kirk … I don't want to," Laura said as she burst into tears.

Kirk rushed over to her side as he noticed that she started crying, "Hey baby, please don't cry," if there was one thing that Kirk hated, it was seeing Laura sad, it was something that always got to him. He embraced her and started caressing her hair in a bid to get her to calm down. His attempt to do so failed because she started crying louder than moments before he held her, "I am sorry, okay?" Kirk apologized again as he wiped her tears.

Laura looked up at him and stayed quiet while trying to stop any more tears from flowing down her cheeks, "I am so tired of fighting baby I am, can we not do this again? I know it is almost inevitable, but can we try not to argue again?" She asked as she looked at Kirk waiting for him to respond.

"Yes baby, absolutely!" Kirk said as he pulled Laura into a hug, just then they heard the kitchen phone start buzzing loudly.

Laura walked over to the other side of the kitchen to pick up the phone. The phone and communication lines had been down and experiencing a blockage ever since the report of the more possible disasters like earthquakes broke out, so they basically had little or no method of communicating with others ever since then. She wiped off small beads of sweat that started forming on her forehead as she picked up the phone to speak, "hello…," she said as she scanned the room and looked over at Kirk.

"Hiya!" the person at the other end of the phone line responded.

She quickly recognized the voice of the person on the other end of the phone line, "Marie!" She screamed as her eyes lit up in excitement and looked around the room a second time.

"It's been so long," Marie said as she let out a huge and exasperated sigh.

"I know!" Laura responded, "How are you doing? How have you been, how are Lance and the kids?"

"I am not fine…I just hope this all ends pretty soon, We have all just been trying to hold it all in and take each day as it comes, one day at a time, and Lance…Lance is in over his head at this point in time, I have never seen him like this in all the years that I have known him", Marie said as she stopped to clear her throat.

"I have been so worried about you…I was just talking to Kirk the other day and I told him that we had not spoken in a couple of weeks leading up to this moment," Laura said as she rubbed her right hand around her belly.

"I am just holding up…it has not been easy, it has not been easy at all, if I must confess."

"Oh my God!" Laura exclaimed as she cupped her mouth with her hands, "You are going to make me extremely emotional girl…please don't cry," she said as tears started forming in her eyes.

"It's just been a lot and I just needed someone to talk to," Marie said as she cleared her throat again. "I need a breather…I just needed to speak to someone that wasn't my husband, and I knew that the person had to be you, and that is why I tried all I could to try to reach you."

"I don't know what it is that I could say to make it all better…I do not have the right words that could possibly soothe your pain in anyway, but I am just led to pray, I want to pray…do you want to pray with me?" Laura said as she looked up at Kirk who started rolling his eyes in disgust as he walked out of the dining room.

"Yes," Marie replied while still struggling to hold back the tears.

"Heavenly Father, our help in ages past and our hope for years to come, we thank you for everything, thank you for everything that you have done for us…."

"Thank you, Lord," Marie replied without letting Laura finish her sentence.

"We are thankful to you for keeping us alive in this moment, we are thankful for our family and all our loved ones, we thank you for sending your son to die for all our sins. We send our blessings to you Lord, we are now more than ever grateful that you have kept us all intact in such a time as this, we are grateful for such a time like this because we know that you are fully aware of the things that are happening during this time and there is nothing that happens that passes by you".

"Lord we just at this juncture want to commit ourselves unto you. If I am going to be honest and speak for everyone, I must confess that this has been a very difficult time, it has been a very difficult turn of events and I must say that it took me by surprise, but I guess…No, I know, that you are the only one with all the answers and you also know why all these things are happening around us, you are also fully aware of everything, we just want to ask that you send your peace, the peace that no man can give, Lord we just want to ask that you send your unending peace our way".

"In this moment Lord, we ask collectively that you send us your peace…the peace that passes all understanding…," Laura said as she stopped to catch her breath.

James had been making silly noises while she was praying but she was not concentrating on it since they were all just trying to have breakfast. It did not bother her for a while until she paused to catch her breath. She looked over at James as she firmly raised her eyebrows and squared her eyes at him. On seeing his mom, James placed his teddy bear on the chair beside him and continued eating. Miranda let out a soft chuckle as she took a spoonful of eggs to her mouth and she almost spat the eggs out, she covered her mouth with her hands to stop her food from spilling all over the Dining table.

"Amen!" Marie replied from the other end of the phone line while she waited for Laura to continue praying.

"Lord, we do not understand anything that is happening with us and around us. All of this is just so sudden, but we know that you are present with us. We just want to ask that you see us through these things that are happening in the name of Jesus."

"Amen, Lord!" Marie responded as she stopped to clear her throat.

"Dear Lord, we are so grateful for our families, thank you for your protection and preservation, thank you so much for keeping us all together and keeping us as one seemingly united front in the midst of all the chaos and things happening, we also want to thank you for our husbands, Kirk and Lance at this moment, who you have placed as our priests and as the heads of our homes. We pray that you keep them happy and give unto them the right wisdom that they need to be able to keep our families united and happy during these times in the name of Jesus."

"We also ask that you continue to keep them strong, let them not grow weary because of all the circumstances that we may be facing at this moment in time. Lord, we ask that you give them both unwavering strength for the journey at present and for the journey ahead in the name of your son Jesus Christ, please keep them whole, body and mind, may they be continually strengthened for this phase of our lives in the name of Jesus."

"Father we ask that they have the fortitude for this journey and we ask that you take away any discouragement on their way, Father in a way that only you can, please prove to them that you are with them and that you are always there with them every step of the way including at a time like this when they all need you the most…at a time where we all need you the most, please help to always keep them sane and calm no Michaeler what the turnout of events in the future will be, please give them the grace to be able to go through all these issues in the name of Jesus".

"Lord we pray for ourselves and our children…we pray for our babies who may be oblivious of everything that is going on as this is all very new for them, we know that they are your children before they are ours, so therefore, we are committing them into your care, father please take care of them yourself, especially in this season of so much uncertainty, and a time where there is so much chaos, we ask that you please comfort them and see them through this all emotionally and physically, we ask that you send them so much strength to be able to pull through this very difficult situation that we have all been plagued with in the name of Jesus".

"Amen Lord…," Marie said as she responded, "Lord we just ask for your peace, please let us know you are with us every step of the way as we go through the chaos we are facing. We want to feel your mighty presence with us as we go through this season in our lives, it is something that we are collectively facing, so we just ask that you please see us through it all in the name of Jesus."

Laura felt a sense of peace as Marie prayed, it was something that she had not felt in a while, and at the very least she had not felt anything like that ever since they started going through all of the difficult situations that they were going through, she felt the baby move around within her which was another confirmation of the almost too good to be true feeling that she had just experienced. "Hmmm…thank you Lord because you are always there for us when we need you, thank you for sending us your peace, you are a good father, thank you for your grace, and thank you for the privilege we have to be able to call on you when we pray".

"Thank you for always paying heed to all our requests and thank you for always being there for us as your children, we are always assured that anytime that we call on you for your help, you always answer because you always want to help your children out, we just ask that you give us a testimony, one that would last and be there for all the ages to come and that will also serve as enough confirmation of the fact that you are a good God and you know just what we need even before we attempt to ask you, we ask that you be with us and guide us all the time, please be our shield, we do not understand anything that is going on, it is all a mystery."

"Lord please guide us, we are fully aware of the fact that we will not be able to get through this face unscathed without you, we know that you see everything, we know that you also know everything that we are currently facing so lord we ask that you let your presence be known, and please send your peace our way to calm this situation and please give us all round victory. We want you to know that we do not trust any other person to see us through all of this but you and we cannot even bring ourselves to trust anybody but you, which is the reason why we have come to you with all of our fears and our vulnerabilities at this moment and we can only trust you to bring everything to a perfect end. We thank you for answering our prayers and we are assured that you will give us overall victory from all our present struggles in Jesus' name we pray."

"Amen!" Marie echoed loudly as she responded and she let out a small chuckle and sigh at the same time afterward, "I am so happy that I got to do this with you, it was extremely necessary, so I just want to say thank you for being led to do this with me, I needed this because I was starting to go crazy, it has not been easy and I don't know if we will be able to do this anytime soon given the present circumstances, but I know one thing, I know that I am grateful to have you as my friend".

"Aww," Laura said as she cooed at what Marie said, she missed her friend , and it was just fitting that they were able to speak to each other at this very moment when they both felt their worlds falling apart. They were indeed two peas in a pod and their connection was sweet and unique. "I miss you so much, I am not going to lie, I just can't wait to step out of my house again and be able to come over to yours, I pray we will be able to communicate as often as we can, and if we are not able to, just know that I love you and I'm rooting for you, I am rooting for all of us, okay?"

"I love you too, hopefully, we can talk again soon, give my love to Kirk and my other babies," Marie replied.

"I will do," Laura said as the call ended and she placed the phone back on its holder.

"Was that Marie?" Kirk asked as he walked back into the dining area.

"Yes," Laura squirmed as she replied and went over to serve her breakfast, every other person but her was already served and had their breakfast and started their regular chores of cleaning up the house.

"That is so refreshing, it is so good to hear from her after such a long time, it's been so long since I heard that phone ring," Kirk said as he gestured to the phone in the kitchen while taking a huge gulp from his cup of coffee.

"I said the same thing, I was so worried before now, I am just so happy that I got to speak to her again. I am so happy that I got to hear her voice again after such a long time," Laura said while taking a big bite of her pancakes. As she looked around the kitchen and smiled, she gestured to Miranda who was cleaning up the kitchen counters, "you have done an amazing job tidying up the kitchen, this is the best it has looked like in weeks," she said as she grabbed a bottle of water to drink.

"Thank you, Mom," Miranda said as she went over to the kitchen sink to help Mike with washing the dishes.

"So, what did she say? How is she holding up, and how is Lance?" Kirk asked as he continued to drink the coffee from the cup.

"Well, she said that she had been trying to reach me for a while, but she could not because the phones were not connecting, and all the other communication lines were no longer working or even going through. She was not sounding bright which is to be expected, I mean, I do not think anyone will be, everything has just been spiraling out of control. I asked her about Lance, and she said he was not holding up too well, but all in all, I am happy that we got to talk."

Kirk smirked his lips as he replied, "Hmmm…at least we were able to hear from them, and the only thing we can wish for from here on out is that everyone is okay, especially you baby, you have been extremely panicky about late, and I have just been worried about you. I know it has not been easy for you and this pregnancy has obviously gone different from all your other ones so I know how you may be feeling, I know that you are feeling overwhelmed, I just want you to know that I will always be here for you."

"Aww baby," Laura geeked as she stood up to go and meet Kirk where he was standing and she kissed him, "I love you so much, everything that you just said means a lot to me. I am just anxious about everything, I am anxious about this whole situation, it literally makes me lose sleep, it's just been a whole lot to take in these past few days and I do not know how I would have been able to sail through it without you being here, without you and my babies", she said as Kirk smiled and gave her a kiss on her forehead.

"I am so happy that you are happy, that is all that Michaelers to me at the moment, your sanity and happiness", Kirk replied as he put his arms around her, "I am happy that we are all here together…", Kirk paused to clear his throat as he stepped out of the dining room, moments later, he returned with Mike, Miranda, and James, "Alright, I would like for all of us to settle down quickly, I want to have a word with all of us around, and I do not plan to take so much time doing that", he said as he carried James and put him on one of the chairs at the dining table.

"Alright, Dad," Mike and Miranda both said in unison as they settled down while waiting for Kirk to continue speaking.

"So, I just want to start by saying I love you all so much…," Kirk paused as he cupped his mouth with his right hand, his eyes had started welling up with tears.

"Aww Dad, you are going to make me cry," Miranda said as she went over to his side and gently rubbed his back for a few minutes before going back to where she was sitting.

"This has been quite the experience and very unusual, as I dare say that we have not gone through anything like this before. I know that it has been incredibly hard for all of us to go through this whole situation… believe me if anyone would have told me that for this amount of time that has passed, we would be holed up in our house and confined to a particular space for this long…I probably would have given them a black eye".

Everyone in the room with Kirk burst out laughing.

"That makes two of us," Laura added as she let out a soft chuckle.

Mike shook his head as he looked at his parents and observed them, "*these two always make me laugh*", he thought to himself before finally speaking out, "Now, I am not saying this because you both are my parents and you gave birth to me, but you both actually agree to have been made for each other, you both are a match made in heaven", he said as he smiled broadly at them.

"That means so much to me, the way you said that…", Laura said as she went over to Mike and gave him a hug, "Thank you so much my baby boy", she said as she kissed him on his cheek afterward and Mike made a face while trying to wipe her lipstick off his cheek.

"You can do that or whatever else you want to do…", Laura reacted after she saw the expression on Mike's face, "I do not care…I am going to keep smothering that face that I made with kisses for as long as I possibly can and you are not going to stop me", she said as she sat back down.

Kirk laughed as he looked at Laura and then at Mike before he cleared his throat in a bid to get everyone's attention. "Alright, as I was saying, and also as is my usual fashion as of late, I just want to use this opportunity I have to check on everyone and find out how we are all doing, every one of us has been affected in small or big ways by the recent turnout of events, and for all of us we have been affected by this in a huge way".

Laura, Mike, and Miranda nodded in agreement as they watched Kirk speak.

"I know it has affected your mom and I because it is supposed to be one of the happiest moments of our lives seeing that we are having another baby and you all are going to be having another brother or sister but these times are evidently very different from what we are used to…I believe it has affected everyone around us as well and for you both…", he said as he pointed at Mike and Miranda.

"I understand it has also been difficult for you seeing that the two of you had to stop school so abruptly and be forced to stay home for this long. I can only imagine what you both may be thinking and what could be going through your heads now, but I just want you guys to know that I am always going to be here for you. If you need someone to talk to, I know that I may not have the right words but just know that you can always come to me for help with anything that you need."

"Thank you, Dad, we appreciate it," Mike said as he looked over to Miranda and he pulled her into a big hug, Miranda looked at Mike and smiled broadly.

"You are welcome", Kirk replied as he continued to speak, "I want to encourage us to take our safety very seriously during this time if anyone of you should notice anything that is funny or seems off, please do not hesitate to let either me or your mom know about it, you cannot afford to take anything for granted, we will try to enforce some new security measures around the house while we are still made to stay put in here, please take everything seriously and let us know about any of your observations".

"Alright Dad, we will," Miranda nodded in response to her dad's warning.

"Very good," Kirk responded and smiled.

"Alright we can all continue with whatever it was that we were doing," Kirk said as he stood up and went over to carry James who had dozed off while they were all talking.

A few hours later, when Miranda was trying to study in her room, she noticed a vibration, she felt it was not anything serious and she did not want to bother anyone about something she felt was so trivial, so she continued studying until she felt it for a second time, and she came down from her bed and went over to Mike's room.

She was thrown off her feet they hit the ground because of yet another vibration, she could not think of any other thing than to call out her brother's name for help, "Mike!", she yelled while she struggled to stand up from the floor but failed to do so because she was struggling to maintain her balance off the ground, "Mike!" Miranda yelled out again and waited for him to respond.

After a few minutes, she heard her brother call out to her from his room, "Miranda, are you okay?" Mike yelled out while waiting for Miranda to reply.

A million thoughts struck her mind at once, she was not even certain where her parents were at the time. "Did you feel that?" She yelled out after she failed to get up from the ground again.

"Yes! What the hell is that?" Mike asked when he felt yet another vibration.

"Can you get to mom and dad? It seems like they are asleep," Miranda replied as she tried to crawl to the door of her room.

"Alright, it seems to have stopped, I will go and check on them in their room, okay?" Mike yelled out as he replied.

"Alright, I'll be waiting for you...," she responded.

"Okay I am going to go now," Mike said as he walked slowly to the door of his room.

"Mike...," Miranda called out.

"Yes Miranda," Mike responded as he walked out of his room.

"Please be careful," Miranda added as she placed her hands on the door of her room.

"I will be careful, so do not worry, okay?" Mike responded.

"Okay, I hear you," Miranda said as she rested her back on the door of her room.

"Dad, Mom!" Mike yelled out as soon as he walked into his parents' room.

Kirk slowly turned over to face Mike as he yawned loudly, "What is it?" he asked as soon as he saw Mike standing at the other side of the room.

"We felt something…like a vibration," Mike added as he looked at his dad while placing his hands on his waist.

"What was that? What did you feel?" Kirk asked as he sat up on the bed.

"A vibration Dad… from the ground," Mike responded as he folded his arms.

"Wow…another one? That is the second one in what…less than three days," Kirk said as he looked around the room.

"What happened?" Laura asked as she rubbed her eyes and moved around on the bed.

"Babe…guess what?" Kirk said as he looked at her.

"What is it?" Laura asked as she sat up to look at Kirk and Mike.

"Mike said they felt another vibration," Kirk said as he looked at Laura squaring his eyebrows.

"What? Why? How?" Laura said as she frantically got up from the bed.

"Babe calm down!" Kirk replied as he stood to help her in standing.

"Mom, take it easy please," Mike added as he looked at Laura.

"Mike is right, this is not good for you or the baby, try not to get too agitated," Kirk said as he placed his hands on Laura's shoulders.

"I can't!" Laura yelled out as she let out a huge gasp while trying to catch her breath, "Don't you get it Kirk? That is the second one that has happened in less than three days babe…if this is the situation here, God knows what is happening in Ohio…," she said as she started pacing up and down in the room.

"I know all that…but you just need to try and relax, okay?" Kirk said as he stopped her in her tracks while she was pacing around.

Mike quickly grabbed one of the chairs in their room, "Hey Mom, please come and sit here," and when she did not budge, he went over to move her to the chair.

"I know that it is incredibly hard to remain calm, but Mom, with everything going on at the moment, we do not want you to get sick, we do not want any of that please", Mike said as he clasped his hands together and looked at his mom, "So mom please…just try to relax a little bit, okay?"

Laura looked at Mike as she nodded her head slowly.

"Alright, so please just stay here while Dad and I go and check things out around the house, so we know that everyone is okay."

"Okay," Laura responded as she looked at Mike again and slowly stroked his hands.

"We will be back soon," Kirk said as he looked at Mike and they both walked out of the room.

They made their way into the hallway and went to Miranda's room to check on her.

Kirk knocked on Miranda's door as he looked at Mike, "Hey Miranda, are you okay?"

"Dad!" Miranda yelled out as she went over to open the door.

Kirk pulled Miranda into a hug as soon as he saw her, "Are you okay baby girl? Mike told me what happened."

"I was a little bit scared earlier when I felt the vibration, so I called out to Mike, Thank God he answered me if not I would have been a lot more scared than I already was, I also did not know what to think in that moment, since it was the very first time that I had even experienced something like that, I was worried that something had happened with you and mom, I am just so happy that you both are safe, it threw me off my feet and balance, and I mean that literally", Miranda said as she was looking directly into her dad's eyes.

"Where is mom?" Miranda asked, "I hope she is okay."

"Miranda…thank goodness you are okay, when Mike walked into our room and told us what had happened, I became worried…more worried than I have been in a while…," he paused to examine her, "I hope you are okay though? I hope you did not get hurt anywhere."

"Dad, I told you, I am fine," Miranda looked at her Dad as she stroked the lower part of his back trying to reassure him, "There is no need to worry about me, okay? I am perfectly fine…besides, we have more important things to be worried about now."

"I agree," Mike said as he raised his right hand in support of what Miranda just said.

"Alright then, I am happy you are okay, I need to check on James", Kirk said as he walked further into the hallway to James's room, he opened the door to the room and saw that James had been sleeping so soundly while holding his favorite teddy bear firmly, he looked like he had not felt anything because if he did, he would have woken everyone with his cries.

Kirk walked into the room, and he slowly picked James up from his bed and he looked up at Mike and Miranda who were both standing at the entrance of the room, "Let us go," he said as he stroked James's back slowly when he saw that he was trying to wake up fully.

They walked back into the room to see Laura asleep on the chair, Kirk went to their bedside and placed James on the bed before walking back to where Laura was sitting as she slept.

"Hey…wake up," Kirk whispered into Laura's ears as he watched her sleep and wriggle from side to side.

"Baby," Kirk said as he tapped Laura on her shoulder.

"What is it?" Laura replied without opening her eyes.

"Are you okay?" Kirk asked as he began to observe her.

"What is it, Kirk?" Laura asked again as she started opening her eyes slowly.

Laura scanned the room to see Kirk, Mike, and Miranda staring intently at her, "would someone please speak and tell me what the problem is?" she said as she looked around the room wondering where James was, she let out a big sigh of relief when she finally saw him lying fast asleep on their bed. She was already starting to have a panic attack when she did not see him standing with Kirk and her other children at first.

"Everyone is fine, at least, we are all in the same room right now," Kirk responded as he began to stroke Laura's hair, "Are you sure you are fine?" he asked as he looked at Laura.

"You know what Kirk? No, I am not fine! I am not fine so there is no point in pretending that I am," Laura retorted.

"You need to calm down," Kirk said while trying to calm her down.

"No Kirk, I cannot calm down, no one in the history of being told to calm down has ever done so, do you realize how much danger we are in right now, do you know what all of this means?" Laura said as she stood up from the chair, she felt a sharp pain rush through her back, and she sat down on the chair again immediately.

"Ooohhh!" Laura screamed out as she plunged herself back into the chair.

"What is it? What is wrong?" Kirk asked while pacing around in front of her.

"I just felt this sharp pain in my back," Laura moaned as she replied while looking up at Kirk.

"What?" Kirk exclaimed as he looked at Laura.

Miranda ran over to her side and started giving her soft and small massages on her back, "Sorry Mom, I am so sorry that this is happening."

Laura smirked as she responded after taking a few short breathing exercises, "You do not have to be sorry, okay? Please do not be sorry because you did not do anything," she said as she took Miranda's hands and gave her a side hug.

"Alright," Miranda replied as she let out a sigh of relief while rubbing her forehead.

"Just try to relax please, do you want to go to bed?" Kirk asked as he looked at Laura and wanted to help her get up from the chair.

"We still don't have any idea what is going on in Ohio…Kirk, I am worried," Laura replied as she raised her hands for Kirk to lift her up.

"Baby, that should not be a bother for you right now, you need to focus on your health and that of the baby, so please try to rest now," he said as he led her to their bed.

"Dad is right," Mike added as he looked at his mom, he could not hide his expression of extreme fear and worry. He was scared that something much worse than everything going on was going to happen, and the suspense of not knowing what was happening outside North Carolina was starting to get to him.

"Mike, try not to be worried about me, okay? I am going to be just fine," Laura said after she took another look at his face, and he was starting to turn red.

"I…am trying to," Mike said as he replied slowly.

"Just try to make sure your siblings are okay, try to make sure they are all good," Laura replied as she started falling asleep when she found a balance on the bed.

Kirk looked at Mike and Miranda as he placed his hands on his waist and winced, "What is the time now?" He said as he looked at the clock by the top side of the wall in the room, "3:20 PM", he read out and looked at Mike and Miranda again, "Let's just try to give your mom some space for about thirty minutes or more, she needs to get some rest, so let's not bother her for a while, at least until she gets up from the bed".

"Alright Dad," Miranda said as she and Mike walked out of the room, followed by Kirk.

They walked into the living room and tried to check around for anything that might have been altered because of yet another vibration, the one that occurred within hours leading up to that very moment. Kirk had been extremely cautious ever since he found out that there was yet another one within less than three days of the first one happening, and he was not ready to take any chances. All that was on his mind at that moment was how he could successfully keep his family safe, and he was ready to do that no Michaeler what it was going to cost him. He instructed Mike and Miranda to look around the house and if they noticed anything out of place, they should let him know as soon as they saw it, since they had not gotten any new updates from the government, Kirk resolved that he was going to take the safety of his family into his own hands.

Chapter Six

After the second vibration, both Kirk and Laura had been feeling extremely frantic and they had been on their toes all night waiting and wondering when they were going to get an update about what it was that they needed to do next. Laura had asked that all of them, including all the kids, stay put in their bedroom in the meantime, at least that way they were going to be sure of one another's whereabouts in the house.

Kirk stepped out of the bedroom and went to the Kitchen with Miranda coming after him. They decided to make a light batch of breakfast. Kirk was going to make oatmeal while Miranda would prepare French toast and scrambled eggs. Miranda walked to the other side of the kitchen to pick up a frying pan and some eggs. Later, after about fifteen minutes, they walked back to the bedroom with the breakfast spread and started serving everyone individually.

Kirk served Laura a hot bowl of Oatmeal and some strawberries, she geeked loudly as soon as he placed the bowl of oatmeal in front of her.

"Thank you so much!" Laura said as she sharply gave Kirk a hug, "I have been craving oatmeal for a while now."

Kirk smiled broadly as he looked at her and lifted her chin just enough for their lips to meet and then he gave her a kiss, "You are most welcome baby," he said as he clasped his hands together.

"It's like you read my mind, I was just going to find a way to make the oatmeal myself so that I could just satisfy this craving," Laura said as she started munching some strawberries and taking a huge dip in the bowl of oatmeal in front of her.

Kirk laughed out loud when he saw her, "You, my queen, are such a baby," he said as they started making cute faces at each other.

Miranda and Mike made eye contact as she tried to wake James up for breakfast. She was still very worried about everything that happened, and it seemed like, at that moment, she just could not bring herself to be happy or joyful. She felt that it was just Mike who could understand everything that she was feeling because they both went through that traumatizing experience together.

"Are you okay?" Mike mouthed as he looked at her.

She shook her head slightly as she responded quietly, "No I am not."

"We will be fine, okay?" Mike whispered again to her to reassure her even though he was starting to lose the remnants of faith that he had left.

Miranda let out a soft sigh as she propped James up from the bed and carried him to the bedside table in the room and she laced a plate of scrambled eggs and a bowl of oatmeal in front of him.

"Okay come on, eat up," Miranda said as she handed a spoon over to James.

"Thank you," James replied in his baby voice as he looked at Miranda and smiled.

"You are welcome baby," Miranda replied as she rubbed his cheeks softly which caused him to smile broadly, and she returned to serve her breakfast.

A few minutes after they all settled down to have breakfast, they heard a noise coming from outside the house. Kirk guessed that the megaphones may have come on again and he told the rest of the family to listen attentively for any new updates.

"Hey guys, please I want everyone to stay put, it might be an important announcement from higher up," he said referring to the government, he gestured for all of them to settle down in different areas of the bedroom while they listened to whoever was going to address them.

"Good day to every single citizen of North Carolina," the voice from the megaphones echoed throughout.

"It's the mayor!" Laura yelled out as she adjusted herself, "Everyone please try to be quiet so we can all hear what he has to say."

"I would like to appreciate every one of you for your understanding and patience through this difficult phase and season of all our lives. As you may all know, we have been feeling some groundling vibrations for a while, and just yesterday we experienced yet another one, and from all of our documentation and observation, that will be recorded as the second one that we have had in the last three days. We are trying to stay on top of the situation in the best way that we know how to, but it must be enforced that we can only do so much as we have never been affected by this magnitude before…"

"I want to admonish each and every one of us, to keep our faith alive and keep our hope going strong because, in this very trying period of our lives, hope and faith are the things that can keep us together…I would like to also announce that as of this morning, we finally got word from the government of the state of Ohio and they shared that they had declared a state of emergency as a result of being hit and affected by the earthquake as it was earlier predicted, and in juncture, I want to use this medium and opportunity to implore all of us to as usual…take our safety seriously, and also attempt to put our minds at rest by assuring us that the government is working round the clock to ensure the overall safety and protection of the citizens of North Carolina".

Laura and Kirk both let out a loud gasp to express their surprise as they looked at their children.

"I would also like to say, that later today, there will be an emergency state-wide broadcast from our foremost and most recognized news network and we will be getting detailed insights into the current situation of things, and this is pertaining to the recent earthquake that has just hit our neighboring state: the state of Ohio…please be on your guard and stay tuned for the Live broadcast happening later today that I stated earlier, it is my sincere wish that we are all able to pull through this very difficult season and situation in the long run. I remain devoted and committed to all the citizens of the state of North Carolina."

Then after a few minutes, the megaphones went off followed by a loud gawking noise from Miranda, she was struggling with her breathing.

She was gripping her chair so hard and almost started hyperventilating before Mike ran over to her side and held her hand.

"Hey Miranda, what is wrong with you?" Mike asked, trying to hear Miranda speak to him.

"I…I…I'm…," Miranda looked at Mike as she struggled to speak.

"What is it?" Mike said as he looked over to Kirk who ran over to meet them.

"Baby girl…what is the Michaeler," Kirk asked as he looked at Miranda trying to figure out what could be wrong with her. After a few minutes, he snapped his fingers loudly, "She is having a panic attack!" he yelled out.

He tapped Mike gently on his shoulders, "Mike…please do me a favor…please go to the kitchen and get me a cup of extremely warm water…the warmth should be more than the temperature of this room okay?" he said as he gestured to Mike.

"Alright Dad…," Mike said as he looked at Kirk, "I will get on its right way," he said as he walked briskly out of the room.

"What is wrong with her?" Laura said as she peeked her head in the direction where Kirk and Miranda were. She was busy tending to James trying to get him to take a short nap, as he had started being restless right after he finished eating his breakfast.

"It seems like she is having a panic attack…that is the only explanation I have right now about the sudden vibration and every other thing that seems to be happening," Kirk said as he took another look at Miranda as he tried to examine her.

"Is she going to be, okay? Do we need to get help?" Laura asked as she looked at Miranda and back at her husband Kirk as she waited for him to respond.

"Try not to worry baby…she is going to be just fine," he said as he peeked out of the room into the hallway waiting for Mike to return.

After a few minutes, Mike came rushing back to the room as he handed the cup of water to his Dad, "Here you go Dad, this is the cup of water."

"That definitely took a while, don't you think?" Kirk winced as he collected the cup of water from Mike and moved to Miranda's side to try to get her to take some of it.

She was still a bit shaky but not as much as the time when Mike first noticed it, "Here you go…take some water" Kirk said as he placed the cup of water on the end of her mouth so she could drink some of it.

Miranda slowly took small sips out of the cup of water as she struggled with maintaining her breathing, she looked around the room at her Mom, her Dad, and her Brother Mike, and gave a thumb's up in an attempt to tell them that she was a little bit okay now, even though she struggled to speak.

Mike laughed as he looked at his sister, "That's so good to know… you made me worried there for a second," he said as he lowered his head to look at her again.

"Are you better now?" Kirk asked as his hands went to her shoulders.

Miranda raised her right hand and winked briefly; Kirk let out a big sigh as he clamped down on the chair next to her.

Later that day, they gathered in the living room to share some of their remaining snacks together and to just unwind from all the craziness happening in the world around them. It was not long after that the TV in their living room came on suddenly, they knew what it meant because the power to the TV and the other visual electronics they had in their home had been cut off ever since the very first announcement about the asteroid was made.

"Good day Ladies and gentlemen, and all citizens of our beloved state of North Carolina, as you all may know, I am your host for tonight's special and emergency news broadcast, Lori Sage and as usual I am bringing tonight's broadcast your way from my home office…I am reporting live on behalf of the FSN News network about the earthquake scare and the devastating way that it has affected one of our most respected neighbors, the state of Ohio".

Laura asked that they all hold hands together while the broadcast was going to be delivered by the news anchor. She looked around at her husband and then her children, the past few days had already been so much for them, and judging by the look on the reporter's face, the news they were about to receive was not likely to be any better than the ones that they had gotten in times past ever since the very first scary and traumatic experience they had with the descendance of the asteroid to Earth, and in the last couple of days, she had started to feel her faith in God dwindle a lot more than it ever had, she could not bring herself to understand why if God was truly with them, why did they have to go through such a horrendous experience, she kept wondering why bad things such as this one they were faced with had to happen at all.

Chapter Seven

Laura could not stop worrying about what was going on in Ohio. Why was it taking so long to get news on the current situation in Ohio? she thought to herself. Laura was adopted at an early age, but she always knew her birth family was from Ohio, and that is where her heart is still. Just then Laura turned on the news, Kirk and James were asleep, and Miranda was in her room talking on the phone to a friend, so Laura could flip through the channels to see what was going on around the world. Laura's eyes got wider and wider as she watched WXCT news. "Oh no!" Laura covers her mouth, so she won't make any noise. Water was everywhere, people were stuck in their cars, and the water was still rising and rising even at the twelve feet level. "My God, My God, this is Ohio. Cleveland Ohio, Cleveland Ohio," she shouted as she fell back on the couch. Laura started to cry as she looked around to see if anyone in the house heard her shout. Reporter Bon ton James was on the roof of the Statehouse reporting the news. "People please if you can evacuate now and turn your radios on as I myself will have to evacuate my family too." "Jesus!" Laura sighed, as she took a deep breath. "What is going on?" The stores were packed, and some people were not waiting in line to buy food, they were stealing it. Cleveland's airports were packed, as people were waiting to board their flights, it was announced there were no more flights out of Cleveland at that time and none for the rest of the week. It was Monday and Cleveland Ohio was in crisis! Ohio normally never floods at this level. Laura got out her phone and googled it to see.

The 1937 flood was particularly deadly in Kentucky, the deadliest disaster in both Ohio and Indiana was yet another disastrous flood, the 1913 flood. The 1937 flood affected nearly all the state of Kentucky, as well as southern Ohio/Indiana. (https:// www.weather.gov). "Lord, please protect my unknown family in Cleveland!" *Boom, boom* it sounds like a bomb going off outside of Laura's home, just then part of the roof on her house caves in. Kirk and Miranda came running in!

"Kirk, Kirk, where is James!?"

"Oh my God, he is sleeping on the bed!"

Mike hears all the commotion and runs and grabs James off the bed. James wakes up from his sleep with a loud cry. As soon as Mike's feet hit the doorway of the front room, there was a loud crash sounding like a firecracker.

"Get down" Kirk yells, "Everyone! Get on the floor and cover your head." They all get in a huddle on the floor with James and Laura shielded in the middle. The room was silent except for the sound of water leaking from the water tank. It was the water tank that had exploded. The earth shook harder than they had ever experienced. They were thrown from one side of the room to the other. The earthquake lasted for about 15 minutes, but it seemed like an hour. After things had settled Kirk went to the garage to look for boards and plastic to help cover where the roof had caved in. Then he left to go to the grocery store to stock up on food. The Supper Big Bear store was the only store open. Kirk jumped out of his car and ran right into the store only to see a big sign that read CASH ONLY! Kirk took a deep breath, his heart was beating fast because he knew he did not have any cash on him, so he ran out of the store, got into his car, and headed to the ATM machine because the one in the store was out of order. The line was a mile long and the store closed in two hours. People were laying on their horns trying to get through the line faster. Suddenly Kirk saw cars turning around. He whispered to himself, "Thank God, get out of line, I need to make it back to the store in time, gosh," Kirk said while shaking his head and driving up slowly with one foot close to the brakes and the other on the gas. Finally, it was his turn. He pulled up to the machine and there were large words running across the screen saying sorry this machine is out of cash, please call your local bank for other locations and options. We are sorry for any inconvenience this may have caused. The Right Bank is here to serve you.

"No NO! YOU ARE NOT HERE FOR ME TODAY!"

Kirk yelled! The car wheels squeaked and there were black tire marks trailing behind the car as he sped off and headed back to the store. When he arrived at the store the parking lot was nearly empty. What is going on? Kirk thought to himself. They were closing in twenty minutes, and his friend who worked there was nowhere in sight. Kirk went to the customer service desk, "is Bill still working," he asked the clerk. Bill heard his voice and came from the back and walked around the desk to greet Kirk. "Hey man, I hate to ask you this, but do you have any cash on you that I can borrow?" "Sorry Kirk" Bill said as he held his head down.

"Carol and I haven't been able to get any money out of the bank for over a week. Bill turned his hand over so he could see his wrist. "I don't see anything," replied Kirk.

I am a part of the hundred in the experiment. "You see that red spot?"

"I see it now."

"I have the chip." Bill smiled. "No more worrying about money. Look man, I would help you out, but all my funds haven't been uploaded yet, please send Laura and the children my love."

"I will, I sure will!" he sighed aloud.

Kirk rushed out of the door bumping into a man on his way out without even saying he was sorry. "Will I have to get this so-called chip in order to feed my family?" God forbid, he spoke out talking to himself not caring if anyone heard him, or not. Kirk's drive back home to his family was long and dreary. Facing Laura and his children was not something he wanted to do.

Kirk was greeted with Laura's expression of silence as he walked into the living room.

"What's up?" Laura asked as she looked at him.

"Nothing," Kirk responded as he collapsed on a chair on the side of the living room facing the front door.

Laura walked up to him as she tried to stop herself from having an outburst, "What do you mean by nothing, Kirk?"

Kirk cupped his forehead with his right hand as he looked at her, "Look babe, I do not want to fight with you, okay?" he said as he sat up on the chair.

"You just went over to the store, right?" Laura asked as she waited for Kirk to respond, "So explain to me…why did you come back here empty-handed?"

"Laura calm down, okay? There was nothing I could do, on my way to the store, I tried to get some money from the bank, but I could not, so when I got to the store, I tried to look for Bill to see if I could borrow some money off him to buy some food and house supplies, but he said he did not have any money on him".

Laura snapped, "So what…you just drove back home with nothing, are you kidding me?" at this time, Laura started to feel her hands shaking.

Kirk stood up and went over to meet her when he noticed the sudden vibrations in her hands, "Look, I have told you before, try not to get yourself worked up over nothing," he started to embrace her.

Laura struggled to release herself from Kirk's grip as she slapped him, "are you telling me all this is nothing? Have you looked around you for a minute Kirk? Like have you stopped to look around you, the world is ending, I am pregnant, and I don't even know if I and the baby are going to make it out of all this madness alive, we barely have any food to eat, and we barely sleep, even when we do, we sleep with our eyes open…".

"Baby, take it easy okay," Kirk said as he massaged his cheeks.

"Are you kidding me Kirk," Laura said as she stopped to catch her breath.

"Alright…I'm sorry, we just have to make do with and manage the food items and house supplies that we have left for the time being, just until we are able to find a permanent solution to all of this", he said as he led her to the couch and tried to pacify her, "Just breathe, it might not look like it, but everything will be fine, all of this will be over soon, sooner than you think".

When he saw that she had become quiet again, he felt that it was the right time to bring up his talk with Bill while he was at the store, that was the first thing he wanted them to talk about before they had yet another argument. Kirk let out a sigh as he started to speak, "So…about Bill…."

"What about Bill?" Laura asked him in a much calmer tone.

"He got the chip!"

"What? How could he do that?" Laura asked wondering how Bill could have given in so easily, he was one of their trusted friends, who had a staggering amount of faith in God, one that was so palpable and caused her to often question, if she had any faith in God at all, so hearing that he had gotten the chip was sort of a big surprise to her.

"He said that it was the only way that he was going to be able to fend for his family and also get some money for his upkeep as well while he was working at the store," Kirk winced as he stroked Laura's hands softly.

"Wow, I cannot believe that he would actually do such a thing, Bill was one of the few good ones left."

"Well, can you blame him, given all of the things that are happening at the moment, I would not say I was surprised, I was not expecting that from him, but I am definitely not surprised."

Laura looked at him with her eyes asking him a question she could not bring herself to ask.

"What is it?" Kirk asked as he looked at her wondering what caused the shift in her mood yet again.

"Is there anything that you would like to tell me, Kirk?" Laura knew her husband way too well for him to pretend that something was not on his mind, and she felt that something was wrong with him.

"Nothing is wrong babe…I am fine," Kirk replied in a slowly paced tone.

"I can tell that there is something wrong with you, so spill," Laura said as she adjusted herself on the couch, refusing to take no for an answer, she tapped him lightly on his thigh as she looked at him, "Alright, I am all ears, what is going on?"

"I do not know why, but I just feel scared babe, I am so scared, I am worried about us and everything going on at the moment, it's just so unexpected," Kirk said as he bowed his head.

Laura looked at her husband and smiled softly at him before she asked, "What are you scared of? Why are you scared?" she said as she lifted Kirk's head so that they could look at each other.

"I am scared of losing you, of losing our babies," Kirk said as he placed his hands on Laura's rounded belly.

Laura smiled as she looked at him, this moment right here was one of the many reasons why she fell in love with Kirk, his ability to be vulnerable with her and tell her exactly how he felt about anything, "Are you thinking about getting it?" Laura asked, waiting for him to respond.

"About getting what?" Kirk asked.

"Are you thinking about getting the chip?" Laura asked as she looked at him.

"Well, the thought never once crossed my mind, given the conditions required to get that thing in the first place, well not until…," Kirk paused as he collapsed on the chair that he and Laura sat on.

"Not until what?" Laura asked as she adjusted herself on the couch.

"Not until I saw Bill today, he looked like he was at peace, and in comparison, with everyone at the store, he looked the least worried or scared, it just got me thinking," Kirk replied.

"So, do you want to get the chip now?" Laura asked as she looked at her husband and stroked his head.

"No…no, I don't," Kirk let out a sigh of relief as he kissed Laura's forehead.

"So, what do you want to do?" Laura asked as she looked at Kirk and pulled him close to her so she could hug him.

"I don't know babe, but what I do know is, I do not want to get that chip. I don't want to have to reduce myself or stoop so low just so I can make a statement. I am not going to do that."

"So, what do we do now?" Laura said as she tried to stand up from the couch.

Kirk moved his hand around the small of his back, he proceeded to take Laura's hand and began to rub it, "The plan is simple, for now, I think we just have to wait. We just must wait and see what is going to happen from here on out."

"Alright…I am with you on that one, we just have to hope for the best and wait we shall."

"Where are the kids?" Kirk asked as he looked around the living room and saw that it was just him and Laura that was anywhere in sight.

Laura let out a soft laugh as she shook her head, "They have been holed up in the room all morning refusing to step out, we have all been in the room all morning actually, waiting for you to get back," she said as she started walking to the room.

"Aww my poor babies," Kirk responded as he walked behind her, and they both made their way to their bedroom.

"So, has the leakage stopped?" he said as he walked into the room and started examining the leakage from the roof.

"Fairly, it just stopped for a bit, like only a while ago, just some minutes before you."

Kirk stepped out of the room again and returned a few minutes afterward with some pieces of wood and some tools in his hands, he rolled up his sleeves and took one of the side stools to climb and access the affected part of the roof.

"Mm-hm!" Laura exclaimed as she watched Kirk work.

"What?" Kirk whispered back to her as he looked at the kids and noticed that they were all fast asleep on the bed, "Don't wake these kids up please."

"You know what? You are mighty fine, Mr. Kirk, can I please have your number?" Laura geeked as she admired him.

Kirk laughed so hard, he started to tear up, "I see that you've got jokes, you are quite the firecracker Mrs. Robins," Kirk said as he smiled and came down from the side stool and went over to her.

"I just love you so much, Laura said as Kirk kissed her.

"I love you too…way too much than I could possibly imagine," Kirk replied as he kissed her on her cheek and placed his hand on her belly and stroked it.

"How is my baby doing?"

Laura let out a loud grunt as she responded, "You know what? This child is about to get on my last nerve, he or she has been moving around in there like crazy. I am so tired."

"I know…I know that you must be tired, I'm sorry," he said as he let out a soft moan and kissed her forehead.

Laura looked at him, with her eyes sparkling so brightly, she admired her husband, and this admiration grew even more during this particularly hard period, aside from God, she did not think she would have been able to survive up until this very moment without her husband being by her side.

"Thank you…," Laura said as she took Kirk's hand.

"For what?" Kirk responded inquisitively.

"Thank you for just being here…", Laura paused as she looked around the room at her kids, "Thank you for being here for me, our unborn baby, and the kids, I am so grateful for you, and I just wonder what I would have done without you, I wonder what would have happened if you were not here with all of us, it would have been so difficult, thank you for always…for always protecting me, for always protecting me and our babies".

"I love you so much," Kirk said as he and Laura had a long hug.

"It is not going to be easy, but as long as we are together, we can overcome anything," Kirk said as he looked at Laura.

Later that day, when the kids got up from their nap, Laura got a sudden call from her friend Marie. They had not spoken in a while nor had the opportunity to talk after their last conversation, which was a long time ago.

"Hi Laura…," Marie said shakily over the phone.

"Hi Marie, you have been on my mind these past couple of days, how are you doing?" Laura asked while signaling to Kirk who wondered who she was on the phone with.

"Something's wrong Laura, something is wrong with Lennox…," Marie said referring to her one-year-old daughter while she fought to hold back tears.

Laura felt her jaw drop, she was expecting Marie to call her with some sort of good news, one that would give her some hope that, at the very least, they were all going to make it out of this current ruckus alive. "Oh my God…,' she said as she covered her mouth with her right hand and held the phone with her left hand.

"What is wrong with Lenny?" Laura asked, waiting for Marie to respond.

"I don't know Laura and that is what makes me so scared," Marie responded as she started sobbing uncontrollably.

"Alright, here is what we are going to do, try to breathe okay…take a deep breath," Laura replied.

"Alright…," Marie responded, Laura could hear her taking short and deep breaths on the other side of the phone.

"So…where is Lance right now?" Laura asked.

"He is in the living room…we have been trying to get in touch with the emergency response team all morning, but it has not been going through," Marie responded.

"Oh…what's happening now, what's the situation there like?" Laura wanted to know what exactly was going on and how she could help.

"Okay…first off, her skin just turned red, she first had a high fever very early this morning…," Marie paused as she fought to catch her breath.

"Alright…just breathe," Laura said when she noticed that Marie started crying again.

"What else is going on?" Laura asked.

"Alright, she has some red spots all over her body, they look like big boils, I don't know what to do Laura, I am so confused," Marie winced.

"Has Lance been able to get through to anyone now?" Laura asked as she signaled to Kirk to come over.

"What is going on?" Kirk whispered as he walked over to her.

"Lenny is not feeling well," Laura whispered as she replied.

"Oh my God," Kirk said as he settled down on the couch next to her.

"We are still trying to get in touch with someone on the emergency response team, but they are still not reachable," Marie said amidst loud sobs.

"Have you tried any of the hospital's emergency contacts?" Laura asked.

"I tried the one from Rebought, but the phone kept declining the call," Marie replied.

"Oh, so what are you going to do now, is her fever still high?" Laura asked as she held Kirk's hand firmly.

"Yeah, it is," Marie replied.

"Have you given her any drugs?" Laura asked.

"I gave her some aspirin drops…the last bottle that we have left in the house," Marie replied.

"Okay here is what we are going to do, while we wait for the line of the emergency response team to come back up and be operative…," Laura paused.

"Alright, what do you want me to do?" Marie interrupted her as she stood up from beside Lennox and started pacing around.

"First…I am going to need you to calm down," Laura said softly.

" Alright…," Marie responded with a shaky voice.

"Are you calm now?" Laura asked as she continued to hold Kirk's hand, she looked up at him and she smiled.

"Yes…I am…yes, I am calm," Marie said as she began to take a few short breaths while waiting to hear from Laura.

"Alright…please get a very dry towel, with a bucket that has mildly cold water in it, what you are going to do is, lightly dab Lenny's body with it starting from her forehead, and down to her hands and legs, do that for about ten to fifteen minutes okay, you have to be careful because of the big boils since we do not know what they are yet".

"Okay thank you so much, Laura, thank you so much for being there for me, it means so much to me…it means the world," Marie replied slowly.

"You are so welcome my friend, you would do the same for me if I was in need, I am just so happy that I can be there for you in this trying time, and I hope and pray with all my heart that Lenny starts to feel much better soon", Laura replied as she looked at Kirk who was now gesturing to her to give him the phone.

"How is Lance by the way, how is he holding up?" Laura continued as she ignored all of Kirk's initial gestures.

"He is such a champ, he has been strong for the both of us these past few days and has managed to hold everything down for us both and the family ever since this whole issue with Lennox started," Marie said as she once again began to hold back tears.

"Aww…don't cry…I know it is extremely hard right now for you, given the current circumstances, but try to be strong my friend…I am praying for you, okay?"

"Thank you so much, Laura, you don't have to do this, but you did and that makes all the difference, I loveI lover that," Marie responded.

"Kirk would like to speak to you and Lance as well if that is okay," Laura said after finally giving in to Kirk's demands.

"We would love that," Marie said.

"Alright," Laura said as she gave the phone to Kirk.

"Hi Marie, how are you holding up?" Kirk asked as he took the phone and heard Marie's voice on the other side of the phone line.

"We are just trying to hold it all together," Marie said as she let out a loud sigh.

"Marie, don't worry, everything is going to be just fine, our dear Lenny is a fighter, she is going to get through this," Kirk said, trying to reassure her.

"Thank you so much Kirk," Marie responded as she thanked Kirk.

"Can I speak to Lance? Is he nearby?" Kirk asked.

"Yeah, he is, please hold on for a while, let me go and give him the phone," Marie said as she walked from where she had been standing and she went to give Lance the phone.

"Hey brother," Lance said as he picked up the phone from Marie.

"My brother!" Kirk exclaimed excitedly, "How are you doing?"

"I am obviously going to be lying if I said I was good, given the current situation of things," Lance replied as he stroked his forehead back and forth with his right hand.

"I can't pretend like I know what it's like…I can't pretend that I know the slightest of what you are going through, but what I can manage to tell you at this moment is…it is going to be alright," Kirk replied.

"Thank you, man, for this call, I was looking forward to hearing from you, this call just happened right on time," Lance responded.

"You are welcome," Kirk replied.

"Have you been able to get in touch with any of the emergency response teams now?" Kirk inquired.

"No, I have not been able to get through to anyone, and I tried all the numbers that I know, I have been dialing all these numbers for the past hour but there is still no response, I really do not understand why, today of all days, they all decide to go ghost on me."

"I hope there will be a response from at least one of them soon, will you call me back in like an hour just so I can know what is up?"

"Alright, I will do just that," Lance said as he ended the call.

The following morning started like all the other days which no one is considered normal again after the crises happening with the world started, Laura could barely sleep the night before because she kept wondering what had been happening all night with Marie and her baby Lennox.

"Have you heard anything from Lance?" she asked Kirk while they both managed to squeeze in coffee for themselves for breakfast while the kids munched on some toast and scrambled eggs.

"No, I have not, and I have been so worried about them, have you heard anything from Marie?"

"No," Kirk shook her head as she responded.

"I hope that they are okay," Kirk sighed as he drank from his hot cup of coffee.

After a few minutes, Laura heard a buzz from her phone, she had placed it in front of her on the kitchen table, she looked at her phone and saw that someone had sent her a text message.

'Hi Laura …how are you doing? We were finally able to get through to one of the numerous response teams last night, they came in and took Lennox…Lance went with them because I could no longer bear to see my baby in so much pain, they claim that it is Influenza, thank God we now know what it is…"

Laura gasped loudly and she looked around the table to see her children and husband staring at her.

"What is it?" Kirk asked her almost exclaiming.

"I got a text from Marie," Laura replied as she smiled at her husband in excitement.

"So, what did she say?" Kirk asked, waiting for Laura to reply to him.

"She said they were finally able to get in touch with an emergency response team last night, and they came over to take Lennox and that Lance went with them," Laura replied.

"Oh…that is great news, right?" Kirk responded.

"Apparently it is…thankfully, they were finally able to get through to one of the response teams, now we will just keep the faith and pray that everything will be over soon enough."

"Yeah, I hope so too," Kirk responded as he kissed Laura on her hand and her forehead.

Pastor Brent and Pastor Mike had been in the church house with their families ever since the news of the meteor coming to Earth was announced. They both thought that it was better for them to remain there until all the crisis that they had been experiencing for a while was over.

Pastor Brent called Pastor Mike into the church's main office for a brief meeting on how to keep the church going despite the ongoing difficulty that everyone was currently facing and to come up with a plan on how they were going to govern the church after the crisis came to an end.

"How are you doing Pastor Mike?" Pastor Brent asked as soon as he walked into the church office.

"The Lord has been merciful to me and my family, even despite all that is currently going on in the world, I am still alive, so I am really grateful," Pastor Mike replied.

"That is great to know…the Lord has indeed been kind to us despite it all," Pastor Brent affirmed.

"Yes, he has," Pastor Mike said as he nodded.

"So quick one, I wanted us to have a meeting about how we can keep the church going in the midst of this crisis and also thereafter, this has already affected the church and impacted it in a very grave way, so I wanted us to come up with a solid plan on how we can properly govern the church at least, when all of this is finally over".

"The spirit is indeed one Pastor Brent, I was also thinking the same thing and I thought of coming to see you much later so that we could properly discuss it," Pastor Mike replied.

"Oh, that is great…," Pastor Brent said as he nodded in agreement, "So what exactly do you have in mind?" Pastor Brent responded.

"While I was meditating in my room a few days ago, I was able to write some of the things that I thought about down so that I could properly present them to you," Pastor Mike added.

"Alright so can I see them now?"

"Of course, you can see them…please give me a minute let me go and get the journal that I wrote them in," Pastor Mike replied as he stood up and started walking out of the office.

"Alright," Pastor Brent responded as he gestured to Pastor Mike.

It had been ten minutes since Pastor Mike walked out of the office. If anything, Pastor Brent hated being kept waiting, he always considered time as something that was precious and priceless and should not be wasted. He looked frantically at the wall clock and then back at his wristwatch,

After another five minutes passed, he annoyingly walked out of the office into the hallway and stopped in his tracks when he saw Lady Bernice, Pastor Mike's wife.

"Hello lady Bernice, how are you doing today?" Pastor Brent asked.

"I am doing very well Pastor Brent, thank you for asking," Lady Bernice responded.

"Is Pastor Mike still in your room…?" Pastor Brent asked, "I have been waiting in the office for him for the past fifteen minutes."

"Mike is not in the room, Pastor," she replied as the expression on her face grew longer.

"What do you mean by that? How can he not be in the room? He walked out of the church office fifteen minutes ago after saying he wanted to get something from the room…something that he wanted to show me."

"I am sorry Pastor Brent; I have not seen him since he first left for your office. I was just on my way to your office to tell him that lunch was ready and invite you both, I have not seen him since then."

"Then we just have to start looking for him…when did you last see my wife?" Pastor Mike asked frantically.

"I saw her about twenty minutes ago when we both finished preparing lunch and afterward, she left the kitchen," Lady Bernice added.

"And you have not seen her since then?" Pastor Brent grew more confused.

"That is real creepy," Pastor Brent hurriedly replied as he began searching all the rooms in the hallway without any sign of Pastor Mike or his wife, Lady Harriet. He walked out of the hallway into the church's main premises, his wife had loved spending more time in the church auditorium, so his first thought was to go and look for her there.

He walked into the church auditorium followed by Lady Bernice.

"Have you seen Pastor Mike or Lady Harriet?" Lady Bernice asked one of the members that she found tending to the church. She also noticed that the church had become a little scantier than when she first got there in the morning.

"No, I have not seen any of them, Lady Bernice," the member replied as he continued to clean the pews in the church.

"Alright. I also noticed that there are fewer people in the church than there have been since morning, do you mind telling me where the rest of them went?" she asked as Pastor Brent walked up to them.

"That is not possible!" Pastor Brent yelled as he looked at him, he was starting to get furious.

"I am telling you the truth right now Pastor Brent, I just came in from the church lodge."

"Don't tell me this is what I think it is…," Pastor Brent exclaimed as he held his chest, he felt a sharp pain in his chest that gripped him.

Lady Bernice paused for a while before she was able to grasp anything of what Pastor Brent was saying, "Oh my God, rapture just took place!" she said as she held the handle of one of the church chairs.

"Oh, dear Lord!" the member screamed as he collapsed to the floor.

"I cannot believe that this is what is happening, oh my God…I have sinned and fallen short, and I can only ask for your forgiveness, please have mercy on me Lord, have mercy on all of us oh Lord, please just this one time if it is not too late, please forgive all your children", Pastor Brent yelled out.

"Oh, my savior, please do not forsake me in my time of need. You are my strength like no other, dear Lord, please do not leave me," one of the members left at the further end of the church yelled out amid heavy tears.

Later that day, the government set up a wide news broadcast for emergency announcements about the latest updates on the worldwide crises and everything that had been happening around the world, with the most recent happening to be the disappearance of some believers.

Laura had not been herself at all these past couple of weeks and she just wanted a breather. She was not particularly sure of what was going on in the world now, and she felt and thought that none of what was happening was natural or normal. She tuned in to the news channel after she heard the announcement of a state-wide broadcast and she gestured to Kirk to come and join them as they listened in.

"Good day everyone I am Bernard Firke, and I will be reporting the wide news coverage…it has now been brought to our notice that in recent times, particularly in the last twenty-four hours, there have been a deluxe of notable disappearances of people across diverse age brackets…"

Kirk let out a huge sigh as he looked at Laura who was starting to look numb, "That is something, what could this be, I wonder what we should expect next because all of these is just simply crazy to me", he said as he looked at Laura and looked back at the TV screen.

"It appears that rapture or something like it must have taken place, but we are still in the middle of finding out for sure if that is truly what it is and not something entirely different, we hope for the best in all of this…" Just then Bernard's co-host Kate chimed in, "Rapture, Rapture". "My God Rapture? You must be kidding. I know you are not insinuating that the rapture is taking place. I am no bible-thumping Christian, but surely if the rapture had not taken place, God would not have left me behind!" Bernard sarcastically responded to Kate. "Bernard, it is unprofessional to upset the world with your personal views. How dare you spread your nonsense among the people in the world."

Chapter Eight

It was so quiet in the house that you could hear a pindrop.

Laura went to check on Miranda, James, and Mike. "Oh, no! My God! Kirk, Kirk!" Laura yelled frantically. Kirk came running to Miranda's room, he looked down on the floor and saw a blue shirt, black pants, black underwear, a black bra, and blue shoes in the middle of the floor. Kirk clasped on the floor as Laura ran to Mike's room and pulled the covers on his bed back. "Jesus, Jesus, did you take my babies and not us? It is me, Laura, I grew up in church. I read and study the Bible all the time with Marie. My Lord, how can you leave me here like this? Are you not Christ, my savior?" Laura fell to her knees weeping hysterically. Kirk came into the room and saw the covers pulled back where his son was lying in bed. Nothing was there, but red night pants, and white underwear. There was no sign of James at all. Kirk fell to the floor, "Lord, you left me here, I am no Saint, but why God, Why Laura? Father, please forgive us, Father, FATHER, FATHER!"

Kirk screamed as sweat and drew poured out of his mouth. Laura and Kirk laid prostrate on the floor pleading to God for forgiveness all night. The next day there was no light, only darkness, and there was an Eerie feeling in the air. It felt like peace had left the world. The days seemed like night and night seemed like day. Food was scarce and there was barely enough water. Laura had been sipping on a cup of water for an entire day trying to savior their water supply. Laura began to feel sharp pains in her stomach as the baby knotted up in a ball trying to survive in her wound. All Laura could think about was the scripture that says pray that your flight doesn't be in the winter and pray that you are not with babies that suck.

But woe to those who are pregnant and to those who are nursing babies in those days! And pray that your flight may not be in winter or on the Sabbath. (Michaelhew 24:19-20)

Kirk and Laura lay helplessly on the floor for three days. Suddenly, Kirk jumped up from the floor and helped Laura up.

"Baby, I have an idea, I need to see Bill. He has already taken the chip. I know he has a good supply of food, and plus, he works at the store. I will drive to his house and get us some food."

"Kirk, do not you dare leave me alone! I cannot bear to lose you too!"

"Do not worry Laura, there is a loaded gun in the closet. If someone comes in here, you blow their brains out! It is you or them, I cannot bear losing you Laura, but you are too weak to travel. You are due in a couple of months, and you are too weak due to not eating full meals. Thank God my phone is fully charged, and Bill only lives about five miles away. I will call you Laura when I arrive at Bill's house." Laura nodded her head as she could barely keep her eyes open. Kirk went to the garage to start the car. He noticed he had six five-gallon cans of gas stored in the garage. Kirk realized it was dangerous to keep gas in the garage, but he had been storing supplies for a few months in preparation for any disasters that may occur. Kirk got in his car and backed out of the driveway while whispering a prayer for Laura and his unborn child. "Lord please provide a way of escape for us." As he drove to the end of his street he could see cars lined up trying to get out of the neighborhood. It was dark and all you could see was bright headlights. It took Kirk 45 minutes just to get off of his street.

As he got closer to Bill's house, he could hear gunshots. He picked up the phone and called Bill,

"Hello."

"Bill, I will be pulling up on your street in five minutes, is it safe to come that way, man? I am hearing gunshots."

"Yes, man I got my camera's running and my automatic shotguns ready to fire at any intruders. What you hear are people letting off warning shots to protect their homes. Kirk, just come to the back door when you get here." Bill was pretty wealthy, not only was he the manager of Super Bear, but he also owned half of the store by investing and buying stock. He had the biggest house in his neighborhood. His house sat on the top of the hill with a winding road that led to it with a huge metal and stone gate surrounding it. Bill had housekeepers and workers who took care of his property.

"Wow," Kirk said to himself, "this guy doesn't even need to work. He has it made, and he has the chip!" Kirk followed the winding road all the way to the back of Bill's house. As soon as he pulled up Bill texted him on the phone.

"I see you Kirk, come in the door is unlocked."

"Ok, just let me phone Laura first and let her know I am here."

Kirk picked up his phone to call Laura as he walked up to the door. The phone just rang and rang, as he walked up to the house.

"Well, hello," Bill said as he opened the door with a big bright smile.

"Bill, how can you smile at a time like this?" I really need your help man." Lauren is with child, and she is starving."

"I will do all I can to help you, my wife is already gone."

"Gone, Gone where? Gone where!" Kirk stumps his foot hard and then jumps up and down. "I

asked, gone where?"

"She is in heaven or on her way there," Bill said calmly.

"How can you be so calm?" Kirk's face turned Beak red.

"Well Kirk, you see, I choose riches over God. I am indeed a believer; I know God is real but I choose to have my heaven here on earth. Don't be fooled, I knew exactly what I was doing when I chose to receive the chip in my wrist."

"No, No, do not say that!" Kirk yelled and fell to his knees.

"Get up, what are you here for?" Bill pulled Kirk up by his shirt.

"I need food and water, and any supplies I can get."

"I will get you enough food and water for two months. I will also give you two dogs and a supply of dog food for two months."

"I don't want the dogs!" Kirk yelled. "Thanks, but no thanks I have enough to worry about."

"Kirk, you listen to me well. I have given you enough food and supplies to last you for two months until Laura delivers the baby, but after two months your supplies will run out and you will then have to use the dogs for food. Now I will follow you home in my truck because I also have medical supplies for you. I have everything you need for two months. After then God help you, you will either take the chip or lose your life. I will not risk what life I have for you. The government will torture and kill anyone who helps those who do not have the chip. I know I am going to spend the rest of eternity in hell, but I am in heaven now, because I have everything I want and need." Kirk walked to his car and Bill loaded up all the food and supplies as he promised him and followed him to his house. As Kirk drove in silence he kept hearing the scripture over and over in his mind, *What does it profit a man to gain the whole world and lose his soul.*

Kirk screamed out loud, Not, me, Not me,

"For God I live and for God I die!"

Then, he heard another voice in his head,

"Why haven't you lived for God a day in your life."

All he could hear was voices as if he had become schizophrenic. The ride home seems like it lasts forever.

Chapter nine

Kirk pulled into his driveway as fast as he could. He barely had the car in gear before jumping out. Bill pulled in right behind him and started unloading the food and supplies into the garage. Kirk shook Bill's hand, thanked him, and headed into the house, as he began to shut the door Bill grabbed the door with a smirk on his face.

"I want to look at Laura."

"What!" Kirk responded sternly.

Bill ran over to the couch to greet Laura. He bent down and whispered in her ear. "I will take care of you when the baby is born. If you don't take the chip, you take care of me, and I will take care of you." Bill kissed Laura on the cheek. Laura was asleep and too weak to even understand what Bill was saying. Kirk grabbed Bill and took him outside.

"What did you say to my wife, man!"

"Your wife is beautiful and might just be your ticket beyond two months. Sorry, Kirk, it is every man for himself. My wife is gone, I will never see her again. I am lonely, think about it."

Kirk raised his fist, and Bill caught it in midair.

"Never bite the hand that feeds you." Bill started laughing. "I am just playing with you, man. I have my neighbor Sarah who lost her husband last night too, so we will take care of each other."

Bill rushed to his car, and Kirk gritted his teeth together as he thanked him again.

After Bill drove away Kirk went into the garage, opened the freezer, and took out a steak. "I will make a good dinner for Laura and I. Steak potatoes and broccoli."

Kirk prepared food and sang in the kitchen while Laura was fast asleep. He put a tablecloth on the table and turned on the radio to some easy-listening music. When the music started playing it startled Laura and she woke up. She could see Kirk setting the table from her prevailing vision. Kirk walked over to Laura and grabbed her hand.

"Dinner is ready my dear!"

"Dinner, my goodness Kirk. Thank God, I dreamed Miranda and Mike disappeared."

Kirk held his head down.

"I am afraid you weren't dreaming; they are gone, Laura."

Suddenly, Laura fell to the floor.

"Laura, Laura!" Kirk ran and got some rubbing alcohol, put it on a cloth, and put it under her nose.

Laura moved her head from side to side.

"Baby you must eat. Our children are safe. You will see them again. Let us eat, please baby let's eat!"

Kirk walked Laura over to the table.

"Steak, potatoes, and broccoli." Laura smiled, seeing it made Kirk smile. He hadn't seen her smile in three days.

"God is still good through it all."

"Indeed, he is." Kirk chuckled.

Kirk and Laura ate their food and tried to make the most of the bad situation. They gazed into each other's eyes like schoolchildren. Kirk pulled his chair up to Laura and fed her some steak as he rubbed her belly. He then leaned over and kissed her on the cheek.

"Kirk," Laura whispered. "Do not start but I think I am too far alone."

Kirk just smiled and kept feeding and kissing Laura and giving her gentle kisses on the cheek.

After dinner, Kirk washed the dishes, cleared the table, and put away the tablecloth. Laura went to take a quick shower. Neither one of them had bathed for three days in fear of running out of water. Laura could not help it, she had to cleanse herself. She felt dirty and didn't know how Kirk could stand to be close to her. She knew she smelled like sour milk. After Laura got out of the shower she went to bed. Kirk stayed up in the living room listening to the radio.

A public announcement was trying to come through on the radio. Beep, beep, there was a lot of beeping and buzzing. It was so loud it was hurting Kirk's ears. No Michaeler how hard he tried, he could not get the volume to go down. Then suddenly, there was silence then the sound became clear. "Hi, this is Kate, and Bernard, to all those who came to us. The government has selected a group of people who were able to volunteer to get the chip. Our Banks are now closed. Sorry, whatever money you have in the bank will not be available to you." Kate took a deep breath and then there was silence again.

"Please bear with us because this is new to us too. We are getting this firsthand just now." Bernard spoke softly into the microphone. He thought he turned his microphone off, but he didn't. The entire world could hear him and Kate's conversation.

"Kate, are you okay?"

"I did not transfer my money from my bank to my card. What am I going to do?"

I do not think you can use it anymore." Bernard sighs.

"Yes, remember there is a special place government workers and professionals can go to stock up, not everyone knows about it!"

Bernard's microphone produced a static sound which reminded him that he never turned it off.

"Sorry folks stay tuned."

"Are you able to read your prompts, Kate?" No response from Kate. Bernard turned his Mic back on and read the prompts.

"Ok, folks we are back, do not panic, I repeat do not panic!

As of today, the banks are closed until further notice. The President has dispatched FEMA to each city and state to give a week's supply of food and water to each household. We will update you as soon as we are informed. Kate and I are here for you as we are all going through this together. It still has not been confirmed whether we are experiencing the rapture or not or if so if we are now in the tribulation period. There are so many questions. Is this science or God's doing or both, did all this come about because of a meteoroid? Stay tuned and have a good night. Tomorrow we will have scientists James Love and Pastor Frost join us to help us figure out what is going on. Meanwhile, it seems like we are under a dictatorship. Our government has full control. We the people trust them to do the right thing on our behalf. May God help us all." This is Bernard and Kate reporting live from station QX95.

Kirk turned the radio off and knelt on his knees on the floor in silent prayer. All he can say is, "Please God forgive me. I believe Christ Jesus shed his blood and died for me. If there is any hope left at all, please forgive me, and save my soul. Father, please if this is the end times, give me the strength to make it through the tribulation. Please have mercy on Laura and my unborn child. We will not take the chip; we will lay down our lives for our salvation." Kirk felt peace during all the chaos. He crawled to bed next to Laura, wrapped his arms around her, and fell asleep.

Chapter Ten

It was morning, with little lights even though the government had set up bright lights throughout the neighborhood, there was still darkness everywhere. It was so hard to tell the night from the day. Kirk jumped out of bed before Laura woke up and went to their neighbor's house. He knocked on the door, and a dark-haired lady answered the door. She was small-framed with distinct figures. She looked like a model. "Hi, my name is Jenny. Are you Kirk?"

"Yes," Kirk answered with a puzzled look.

"My whole family disappeared. When I arrived, they were all gone, their clothes and shoes laid with no sign of them. There were five sets of clothes and shoes on the floor."

Kirk shook his head. "We have to help each other through this. My wife is pregnant, I am sure you know her, Laura?"

"Yes," Jenny smiled. "How can I help?"

"Our children are gone too, there is going to be a news report today on the radio and on the big screen. I do not want Laura to hear it, maybe you can have a girl's day today? I will bring over some frozen pizza."

"That will work, I have makeup and nail polish."

"Thank you."

Kirk went home and Laura sat at the table eating breakfast. He sat by her and kissed her on the lips gently.

"Babe, Jenny is here. She would like to have lunch with you."

"Great, I haven't seen Jenny in a while."

Kirk and Laura passed the time by talking and laughing. Laura loved to hear Kirk's Jokes. He was an all-around guy, he knew how to be serious when it was time to be serious, but he loved to have a sense of humor. Two hours passed by, and it was noon. Laura headed next door to meet Jenny. They laughed and talked and caught up on old times.

Kirk waited patiently for the radio to come on. There were no signals. The TV started to get fussy, then a picture came in. "This is President Green. I am here to inform you of some good news. Our country is in a crisis, and we have been preparing for this type of crisis all of our lives. I am pleased to announce there is life in space. I repeat life in space. People do not fear, we have a place to go. This world is not and will not be our only home. If the earth is destroyed, we will rebuild. We already have food in space and houses. Right now, we currently have fifty people living in space as we speak. Stay tuned for more information. From what I can tell you, there is no cash in space. We the government will not provide for you long term. You must prepare to take the chip, or you will not. Survive. Anyone who speaks against the government will be mutilated.

We are your God now, we are in charge, but you handle the choices you make. We are trying to build long-term inhabitants underground. There will be levels of comfort just like there are levels of income. Your cooperation and family status will decide where you will live. I repeat, Rapture or not, end times or not we are in control. We knew it was no longer. If there is a God, he will help us all, good night and God Bless America."

Some hours later, Laura came back to the house and met Kirk slumped up across the couch.

"What is wrong?" She asked as she slowly walked to sit beside him on the couch.

"We are being asked to evacuate…" he shakily replied while trying to look at Laura.

Laura's heart started to pound heavily after listening to Kirk.

"No! No! We have been forsaken while the sinner lives comfortably."

The next morning Laura woke up feeling extremely uncomfortable. She had become so overwhelmed with emotions and all the changes that had been happening around her and to her body for the last eight and a half months of her pregnancy and every other thing that was happening all over the world, she was already starting to nurse the feeling that everything was going to come to an end. She was starting to feel more convinced that the world was coming to an end sooner than she had imagined.

It was the first time in eternity that she could no longer control her emotions. She covered her mouth with both hands and started to wait so loud that it woke Kirk from a deep sleep. Slowly she fell on the ground after a short scream. Kirk rushed to the living room and found her lying on the floor.

Kirk ran over to her side and began cradling her, he still had no idea about what to do and the decision to make about whether they were going to evacuate to space or choose to stay underground, he also knew judging from the look on Laura's face that she was in a lot of pain.

Laura shrieked out in pain as she looked at Kirk and then around the room consecutively, she knew from the rushing pain she felt in her back and waist that something was wrong. "What is wrong?" Kirk asked as he looked at his wife.

"I don't want you to worry about anything, I just don't feel too good at the moment," Laura replied as she looked at Kirk.

He stood up and tried to get Laura a cup of water from the kitchen. Laura was in a lot of pain the day before but had mistaken it for Braxton hicks. She had faced a lot of stress during her pregnancy, so she was not sure she was going to be able to carry her pregnancy to the full nine-month term.

Kirk watched Laura from the kitchen stand while he poured out water from a jug into a cup screaming as a result of the unbearable pain that she was now facing, "What is it?" He asked as he rushed over to her. after he heard her screaming. "What is wrong…tell me what is wrong."

"I think the baby is coming," Laura replied as Kirk ran over to her.

"Babe, what do you need, tell me what you need, and I'll try to get it," Kirk replied as he started panicking and began prancing around in circles.

"I need you to try any of the emergency response numbers to see if anyone goes through…," Laura said as she held Kirk's hands.

"Where is the phone?" Kirk asked as he frantically started looking around the house for it.

He began dialing some of the emergency response numbers that they had pasted on the wall of their kitchen in case of any emergencies like this one, but unfortunately, none of the numbers were going through, he paused to look at Laura after a few minutes of him dialing away on the phone for a final time.

"Kirk…we need to act fast…I can't stand this pain," Laura said as she moved her body around in an attempt to ease the pain.

"I have been trying all these numbers for heaven knows how long and none of them seem to be going through, I don't know what to do," Kirk replied as he combed through his hair with his right hand.

"Can you call Jenny, she is a midwife right…," Laura asked as she reached out to take his hand.

"Yeah, you are right, she is…hold on a second let me call her," Kirk replied as he tried to stand up from Laura's side.

Laura prevented him from doing so because she held both of his hands firmly, "Please don't go anywhere, please don't leave me alone Kirk."

Kirk kissed Laura's forehead as he looked at her and tried to wipe the remnants of tears from her cheeks." Look baby, I am never going to leave you, okay? Let me just try to get through to Jenny on the phone. I will be right back," Laura nodded as he stepped away from her.

He picked up the phone and dialed Jenny's number, while silently wishing that the call would go through.

"Hello?" Jenny responded in a laid-back tone as she picked up the phone.

"Hi Jenny, it's Kirk here," Kirk responded in a whisper.

"Oh, Hi Kirk, how are you doing?" Jenny asked as she placed her right hand on her waist.

"My wife is in labor…Laura is in labor, please could you come over and help us out?" Kirk asked as he squared his eyes.

"Oh my God Kirk, of course I will be happy to help, just give me a few minutes and I will be right over," Jenny replied.

"Ooh…thank you so much, Jenny, I really appreciate it," Kirk said as he dropped the phone and rushed back to meet Laura.

"What did she say?" Laura asked as she buried her head in Kirk's shoulders, she was starting to get weak.

After about seven minutes, Kirk heard the front door creak open, so he looked back to check who it was. "Oh Jenny, thank you so much for coming," he said as he propped Laura up so she could sit straight.

"You are welcome…," Jenny replied as she greeted him, "I got here as soon as I could, how is she?" Jenny asked as she walked inside the house, she stopped as she saw Laura and gasped loudly, "why are you bleeding?" she asked as she hurriedly ran over to meet her. She saw that Laura had turned pale and her lips were getting dry.

Jenny hurriedly held Laura because she appeared faint while placing her night coat on the floor, "I am so sorry, I would have been here earlier, how long has she been in labor for?" She asked as she examined the pool of blood.

"She has been in labor for about two and a half hours now," Kirk replied as he raised his hands up in frustration. He looked at Laura and cradled her, she was already extremely weak, and could barely talk, "Alright baby, we are just going to have to deliver our baby right here at home…"

"What?" Laura managed to reply as she looked at Kirk.

"None of the emergency numbers are going through, and I cannot bear to see you like this, your contractions are too close together now to keep waiting on people that may never respond. That is why Jenny is here, she is going to help us," Kirk replied in an attempt to pacify her.

"Alright Kirk…we are going to have to do this together, please for the sake of your wife and your precious unborn baby, please just try to stay with me, your wife needs you now I am going to need some fresh towels, a bowl of extremely hot water, wipes, hand gloves, a pair of scissors and a bottle of disinfectant", Jenny said as she looked firmly at Kirk.

"Alright Jenny, thank you so much for doing this," Kirk said as he scrambled out of the living room to the store to get the items.

"I think I need to push!" Laura yelled out as she grabbed Jenny's hand.

"Just breathe, okay? Try to breathe through it, I am here with you, your husband is right here and I'm going to do all I can for you and your precious baby", Jenny looked up to see Kirk frantically rushing back into the living room with the items that she had asked him to bring earlier on.

Kirk shakily placed one of the towels on the floor as he held Laura who was starting to lose consciousness, he tapped her shoulder lightly and kissed her forehead, "Alright baby, it's go time…you are the most beautiful and the strongest person I know and I love you okay?"

"Okay, when you feel a contraction building, please push okay?" Jenny said as she looked at Laura and tried to help her sit up.

"Jenny, please do all you can for my wife and our baby," Kirk affirmed as he begged Jenny.

Laura nodded and looked at Kirk as she nodded, "Okay," she shrieked out in pain because she could feel yet another contraction. "Baby, you can do this…," Kirk said as she held Laura's hands. "You are doing so good baby," Kirk said as he dabbed on her face with some wipes to remove the big beads of sweat that formed on her forehead. "Oh my God, this is just ridiculous!" Laura yelled after she felt the rush of another contraction in less than three minutes.

Kirk held her head and shoulders as she began to push, her face was extremely red from all the stress and pain she had felt, as she had lost so much blood already, and she was worried for their baby's safety. She looked at Kirk again and saw him smiling so broadly at her as he spoke, "You've got this baby, we've got this," Laura felt a sudden wave of strength as she started grunting and felt her body give way to a very big push. "I can see the head!"-Jenny yelled out. She paused to take a few short breaths as Kirk offered her a glass of water. She looked at her husband and then looked at Jenny at the other side of her body and was somehow able to draw some strength from looking at their faces, she gripped Kirk's hand as she let out the last push.

Kirk burst in tears gasped as he watched Jenny usher their baby into the world, Kirk looked down at the baby and smiled, and looked back at his wife, "it's a girl", Jenny said as he gently cut the umbilical cord and looked at Laura again who was beaming with short smiles as tears welled up in her eyes, "Oh baby, thank you so much for coming out of me", she said as she watched Kirk bring the baby to her.

Jenny smiled as she looked at Kirk and Laura in admiration, she had always been in awe of them both and she admired how they both loved each other so much, she was happy for them, that despite all the pain they had experienced, they finally had something to smile and be happy about, she joined them and they looked at the baby. She was so beautiful, and she had a lot of hair, way more than that of any of the babies she helped deliver on the coast.

She looked at the baby and noticed that the baby's eyes were not open, and the baby also was not crying. She found that to be very odd since crying was something babies did all too well when they are first born, or upon their entrance into the world, "Why is she not crying?" Laura asked as she looked at Jenny and then at her husband. Kirk nodded as he looked at the baby again, "That is true, her eyes are also not open, what could be wrong Jenny?"

Jenny looked at the baby and saw that her nose was clogged with blood, she placed her on the ground where the towel was and tried to remove the blood from her nose as Laura began to cry. She let out a lot of soft sobs as she held onto her husband and watched her friend try to resuscitate their newborn baby. She saw how all her attempts to do so failed one after the other, she had been preparing for the absolute worst of their current situation, but what she was experiencing at this moment was gut-wrenching.

"Save my baby! Please save my baby!" Laura said as she squeezed her eyes shut because she could no longer watch any further horror unfold. She clasped her hands together as she began to pray, "God if you can hear me, please don't do this. Please don't take my baby from me. She does not deserve this, please bring my baby back to me."

After a few more minutes, Jenny looked at her and she knew what that look meant. "I am sorry guys, she did not make it," Jenny said as she placed their lifeless baby on the floor and crawled to Laura's side. "No!" Laura yelled out as she clutched the nape of her robe, "No God, No!" she yelled out as Kirk embraced her and tried to comfort her.

"She can't be gone Kirk, we waited all this time to meet her, what do you mean she did not make it," Laura said while letting out loud sobs.

"I'm sorry baby…I'm so sorry," Kirk said as he stroked Laura's hair while Jenny fought back tears as she tried to hold her. Kirk was trying so hard to hold back his tears as he looked at Laura while she continued sobbing profusely, "It's going to be okay…baby it's going to be just fine, please I hate to see you like this, it may not make sense but it's going to be okay."

"Don't tell me that Kirk…don't tell me that it is going to be okay because it's not. It isn't going to be okay! Why did this have to happen? Why now when we waited so long for her? It does not make any sense. Why would he decide to take my baby away from me? What did I do so wrong?" Laura asked as she looked at Kirk.

"Shhhhh…it's going to be okay, I know I may not be making sense right now, but please know that I am here for you, we are all here for you, I am sorry that this had to happen to us, I don't understand it", Kirk said as he shook his head. He did not realize when he also started sobbing profusely to the point where he could not control himself. He just could not bring himself to embrace the fact that the baby they waited so long for was no longer with them.

"We have to get you cleaned up, okay?" Jenny asked as she lifted Laura from the floor and gestured to Kirk, "Please get me one of your wife's house robes and some paper towels so that we can clean up the blood on the floor, also please can you get me another bowl of warm water…"

"This is all so messed up!" Laura yelled out as she tried to release herself from Kirk's grip.

"You need to calm down baby, try to calm down, okay?" Kirk said as he tried to stop her from hurting herself.

"What more do you want from me?" Laura shrieked, referring to God, "Do you want my life or what? Why did you let this happen? Of all the things you could do yet again… you took my child away from me… my poor baby."

Jenny stepped away to use the bathroom and walked into the living room a few minutes after as Kirk tearfully wrapped their baby in a fresh towel and took her into one of the rooms. She hurriedly walked back into the living room and started cleaning Laura up. By the time Kirk returned, Laura had fallen asleep, the sight of her sleeping relaxed him.

Jenny eventually finished tending to Laura as Kirk continued with cleaning up the living room, he thanked Jenny and then carefully carried her to their bedroom while she slept.

He walked back into the living room and let out a huge sigh while he attempted to hold back his tears. He met Jenny sitting on a couch as she looked at the ceiling quietly. He went over to her and embraced her as they cried together. If there was anything Kirk was looking forward to, it was the birth of this baby, as he felt that it would somehow serve as a glimpse of hope for better things to come, for himself, his wife, and for the memory of their three children, Mike, Miranda, and James.

Chapter Eleven

The next morning after what could be termed '*the worst night of all their lives,*' they got an emergency broadcast alert. Laura managed to walk into the living room assisted by Kirk, Jenny followed them to the living room from behind. Jenny had stayed over through the night just so she could help Kirk keep watch over Laura. They had quietly buried their daughter during the early hours of that morning amidst a truckload of heavy tears and sobs. They buried her in the corner of their backyard just beside their garden, just so they could visit her grave from time to time.

The mayor was addressing the emergency broadcast which was something unusual because he rarely gave such speeches and was seldom seen out in public except for major events or occasions. "Dear great citizens, it is with mixed feelings that I bring this broadcast your way today, I say mixed feelings because I feel both gratitude and sorrow as I speak to you, gratitude because we have finally found a way to keep us all safe from what seems to be the impending end or destruction of the world".

"In this regard, I would also like to announce that the preparations for the evacuation of citizens to outer space and our safety underground structures are now in full swing and effect, and starting this morning, we will begin the process of successful evacuation of all citizens, so I want to implore and encourage us all to cooperate with the government, it's officials and agencies in ensuring a smooth run of this operation", the mayor paused before he continued his announcement.

"All of this that we do is to ensure the safety of all our citizens. My heart goes out to every person who has lost something in the course of this extremely difficult and agonizing journey that we have been going through, individually and collectively we have already lost so much, which is why I feel a lot of pain and sorrow as I can only wish for the best in this very bleak situation and also hope that this pain would go away soon and we all will heal".

"We will begin the evacuation as soon as this broadcast is over, and we will be moving from house to house to ensure this all goes smoothly. Please note that all your needs will be adequately catered to whether you choose to stay in any of our underground safety facilities or choose to be transported to outer space, please start making adequate preparations for evacuation along with your families, as we continue to hope and pray for a better outcome from all the chaos happening in the world at the moment, I am Mayor Brunsworth, and I remain in your service always", the mayor said as he closed his speech and the broadcast came to an end.

"Just perfect," Laura squealed as she looked around at her husband and then at Jenny who was trying to give her a cup of chamomile tea. She had lost all hope ever since their older children disappeared and then they lost their newborn as well, she was not ready or healed up enough to be carried to outer space. She had no faith in the government's ability to provide safe transportation.

"Now there is absolutely no way that I am risking what is left of my life to be transported to outer space, it's not even an option, I am not going to do it," she said as she pointed her fingers in the air to express her disapproval.

"I am also not in support of that babe," Kirk said as he stroked Laura's hands to try to calm her down because he could hear a lot of tension in her voice when she spoke earlier on.

"So, we are going underground?" Laura asked as she looked at her husband while waiting for him to respond.

"Yes, that is the most appropriate option for us to take at the moment, I'm not going to be an experiment all in the name of safety and neither am I going to let my family be a lab rat or scapegoat in all of this madness," Kirk replied as he shook his head.

Kirk clapped his hands as he stood up from the couch abruptly, "Alright then, let us start preparing to move", he said as he gestured to Jenny to follow and assist him, so they could both pack up some clothing and essentials for everyone since that was what they needed because it was said that every other necessity will be adequately taken care of.

Kirk went into the kitchen and started making a bowl of oatmeal for himself, Jenny, and Laura so that they could have breakfast before they were eventually evacuated from their home. A couple of minutes later, the oatmeal was ready, and he served it into separate bowls so that they could all eat.

"Breakfast is ready," he called out to them as Jenny made her way to get some oatmeal, he took a bowl of oatmeal to Laura who sat in the living room looking at the ceiling obviously lost in her thoughts. "Hey babe," Kirk called out to her as he placed the bowl of oatmeal in front of her.

"Laura!" he called out again and snapped his fingers in front of her to grab her attention.

"Babe come on, you have to eat something, you have not eaten anything since yesterday and that is not good for you," Kirk said as he tried to persuade Laura to eat.

"I am not hungry Kirk, I don't want to eat anything," Laura replied, she was sure she was not going to get over the death of her daughter anytime soon. She wished that time would just stop so she could properly process her grief, she unconsciously placed her hands on her belly, and she started sobbing uncontrollably.

"I don't know what to do," Laura said as she covered her face, Kirk and Jenny paused and embraced her and they cried together. There was no one way to process grief, it was unending and carried a whirlwind of emotional and mental breakdowns. Kirk knew he had to do everything that he could to keep what was left of his family, who met himself and Laura in one piece in this particularly difficult phase of their life, he also knew that he had to be there for his wife because out of everyone else, he knew the journey they had to go through to have another baby, it irked him that they had to go through all that hardship.

As they embraced each other, they stood still and each and every one of them tried to draw strength for the days ahead which were going to be extremely unpredictable because the government's resolve to immediate evacuation of everyone from their homes was certainly a cause for alarm.

They heard a knock on their front door in no less than five minutes, Kirk looked at them and started walking towards the front door, "Everyone just stays put, okay? Let me see who it is."

"Be careful," Laura whispered to him as he walked to the front door.

"Alright I will," Kirk replied as he carefully opened the door.

He opened the door and saw two heftily built men dressed in black standing on the front porch, wearing sunglasses. Kirk looked further out and saw some buses parked on the freeway, so he knew that the evacuation process had started.

"Good day sir…," one of the men greeted Kirk as soon as he walked to the front porch, he was holding a tablet and scrolled through it before he looked up again, "Mr. Kirk…I believe?"

"Yes, I am Kirk, how can I help you?" Kirk responded.

"Alright, we are here to assist with your evacuation, as the process is already in full swing, please can you call out the rest of your family and also bring some of your clothes along with you? Before we proceed though, I would like to ask if you would want to be evacuated to outer space or to any of our underground safety facilities?"

"My wife and I, along with our friend Jenny, would like to be evacuated to any of your underground safety facilities," Kirk replied.

"Alright then, that is good to know, please call out the rest of your family members then, we have only five minutes," the man responded as he looked at his pocket watch.

Kirk returned to the living room. He gestured to Laura and Jenny and informed them of the officials' arrival, he then went into their bedroom to start moving their bags of clothes out of the house. Jenny helped to properly secure the house while Kirk led his wife out of the house.

Laura walked onto the front porch and paused to look at the array of buses lined up on their freeway, she looked around to see if she was going to see Marie because her house was just directly opposite theirs, but she did not see her, she noticed that some security officials had been waiting outside Marie's house, but no one came out to meet them.

"Kirk, could you find out what is going on, I have not seen Marie," Laura asked Kirk. He nodded and walked over to the entrance of Marie's house to speak to one of the officials waiting outside.

"Hi, I just wanted to ask what is going on, the owners of this house are our friends and neighbors, but we have not seen them ever since the evacuation started, is everything okay?"

"We went inside their house and back to the front porch, we searched for them around the house, but we did not see anyone. I am afraid they may have disappeared."

"Oh my God!" Kirk tried to control his scream as he covered his mouth. He could not believe that Lance and Marie were no longer with them, he struggled to figure out a way to update Laura about the situation, he could feel his legs wobble as he walked back to their front porch, "They have disappeared", he said as he placed his hands on his waist and let out a huge sigh.

Laura felt her heart drop as she reached out to Jenny to hold her, "What do you mean by they disappeared?"

"That's what one of the officers over there told me," he replied as he pointed at the officers standing outside Marie and Lance's house.

"That is not possible, how did they disappear?" Laura asked as tears dropped from her eyes and she started losing her balance.

"Laura, you have to take things easy," Jenny yelled out as she struggled to hold her.

"Mm-hm", one of the officers said as he cleared his throat and placed his hand on the monitor in his right ear, he paused and then looked around, "We are ready for you, and we have to get going now so we can all take cover before it gets any worse, we have little or no time on our hands at the moment, so it's just best that we get going to the facility right away".

"Alright then…please lead the way," Kirk replied as he looked at Laura and Jenny. "Okay, guys! Let us go," he moved to Laura who at this point was still visibly shaken by the news he broke to her about Marie and Lance's disappearance.

As he led her from the front porch to the van parked outside and watched the ruckus that ensued with a lot of people being escorted out of their homes. Kirk stopped and took a final look at their home, his mind puzzled with a lot of questions, he had reached a place of acceptance that things may not return to normal or go back to the way they were.

A few minutes later, the van carrying them stopped in front of a heavily gated and secure building. Kirk tried to take a look at the building but stopped midway because his eyes could no longer meet up with how tall the building was. One of the officers stepped out and opened the door of the van, "Alright, you are welcome to one of our most secure underground facilities, be ensured of your protection during your time here for however long it lasts, we are always at your service, so I will escort you into the premises right now", he said after he took a bow.

"Thank you…" Kirk replied. He looked over at Jenny and thanked her for being with them, as it meant a lot to them in this tough time. "Let's all go in," Jenny and Kirk smiled at each other as they held Laura's hand and led her out of the van.

"Easy", he said as he walked out holding Laura's hands, she looked around at the property and gasped, "I cannot believe that this is my new reality…all of this is pretty crazy to me, what is the meaning of all of this, I am so tired, just take me already, I am so tired of this misery, take me", Laura yelled out.

"I know how hard it must be for you, my friend…" Jenny said as she held Laura and hugged her tight. "I understand how you feel, but you must just try to be strong, we must all be strong," she said looking at both Kirk and Laura.

"Time is of the essence, ma'am," one of the officers escorting them said as he looked at his pocket watch.

"I miss my babies," Laura said as she clutched her chest.

"We have to go in, so let's go in right away," the officer said as he looked at Kirk.

"We are right behind you," Kirk said as he kissed Laura and held her hand, they began behind the officer. Kirk looked around the facility and was quickly blown away by how the building was structured, he could not help but wonder if it was going to be able to withstand any further disaster coming their way.

The officer turned to Kirk and asked if the three of them would be staying together in one bunker. They all looked at each other, Jenny started to respond when the officer interrupted her,

"I'd say that you are a family winking at Kirk as he continues to explain. "then I would have to give you no less than a two bedroom with 1 ½ bathrooms or two full bathrooms. If you have children or plan on having children, Laura grabbed her stomach, dropped over, and blurted out a loud cry. "I AM NO LONGER PREGNANT!" Kirk quickly covered her mouth.

"It is okay, don't worry, a three-room apart with two full bathrooms it is." The officers pointed to their living quarters and handed them two keys. He led Laura and Jenny the way towards their room. Just as the officer was leaving, he whispered to Kirk, "I won't say a word and know no one will question me as to why I gave you and your family such a large bunker. I am the chief officer in charge. I think you should go to the medical station and get your wife some sleeping pills. Tell them Officer McCauley sent you and you have a spending tab of $500 dollars for the month. Trust me, it should hold you. You will not have to worry about food or other necessities. Our government has spent years setting up this system. I am so glad you picked living underground. When your wife is asleep, come and talk to me. My family and I have an apartment" he laughed "just down the hall number 210." Kirk smiled as he shook his hand, and thought to himself, "201, we are in 201, okay thank you."

"No problem," Officer McCauley responded as he walked towards his apartment. When Kirk closed the door, he saw Jenny holding on to Laura rocking her as she cried herself to sleep. "I'll take it from here," Kirk whispered to Jenny as he separated Laura from her embrace. Kirk gently kissed Laura on the cheek and guided her into their master bedroom. The room was plush with feather-down comforters and Egyptian sheets. The windows were laced with a satin gold curtain with white sheers. As he laid Laura on the bed, he could not help but notice a small refrigerator full of liquor and several types of drinks with a snack bar right beside it. Kirk wasn't a drinker, but given the circumstances, he decided to have a drink, so he poured himself a glass of wine.

Chapter Thirteen

Kirk was overwhelmed and could not wait to meet with Officer McCauley in private. He peeped in on Jenny who was fast asleep. Then he closed the door very lightly and went down the hall to the medical station and picked up some sleeping pills, Tylenol, and acid reflux medication. Afterward, he headed to Officer McCauley's apartment. It was now about 8:30 pm, and he hoped he was not disturbing anyone. He knocked on the door and the officer opened it with a bright grin on his face.

"Come on in buddy, I have been waiting for you. I know you must be frightened and wondering what in the Sam Hell is going on." Officer McCauley said with a stern yet shaky voice. "Like as we knew it, it is no more! This is it, we missed it, WE MISSED IT! I thought I was a good man, Kirk, look at me I am still doing good looking out for you and your family, but being good is not enough. I never believed in that religious stuff, and now here I am."

"What!" Kirk Screamed. Officer McCauley covered Kirk's mouth. "Now, Now, You don't want to do that." Officer McCauley Nodded at him as his daughter came running out of her room.

"Daddy, are you okay?"

"Yes dear, meet Mr. Kirk, he was just laughing."

Kirk greeted the little girl as he tried to keep his composure. The little girl ran back to her room. "Please continue to explain," Kirk motioned to the Officer.

"Behind closed doors, you can call me Ken, but in public, I am Officer McCauley." Kirk nodded his head in agreement. Ken continued to talk. "We are living in unbearable times right now, and our government is taking advantage of it to put in place the New World Order. I am sorry Kirk, but this is just the beginning of sorrow. I know you have heard the saying eat, drink, and be merry for tomorrow you shall die, well that is true. In fact, we all have three months to decide if we take the chip or not. Those who chose not to will die of starvation, sickness, and disease."

"What?" Kirk covered his mouth in disbelief.

"You mean to tell me this all occurred because of some stupid meteor?"

"No son, you got it all wrong. The government has been looking for an opportunity to put a New World Order in place for some time now. God just saw it as the perfect opportunity to remove his people from this world. Next is the tribulation period. Then there will be no believers left on earth. Kirk, I am a believer, and I do hope you are too. We have missed the rapture. This is not a dream. We will have one more chance to get it right, and that is refusing to take the chip and ask God to forgive us of our sins. When we refuse to take the chip some of us will be thrown in prisons, killed and some will starve, but ultimately, we will lose our lives to gain eternal life with Christ." He said "If we deny him, he will deny us. You see I denied him when I refused to accept him into my life and chose to live how I wanted to live. As long as I treated people well, I thought I would make it to heaven. I was angry when I saw my Christian friends disappearing. I even had a friend who was not a Christian at all accept Christ into his life about a month ago. He is gone too Kirk we cannot blame God for the choice we have made. His words are true. I denied him and he denied me. Accepting Christ is a choice. It will not be easy to accept God in a godless world, but I will bow to no one but him. Did you hear the mega speaker announcements saying we are your God Now?"

Kirk shook his head silently.

"Yes, I understand exactly why I was left here, but why Laura? She was always trying to get me to go to church, she would also have Marie and her husband come by from time to time and pray with us. Then when I refused to acknowledge Christ as my savior she stopped going to church and her faith began to waiver" Kirk sighed in dismay.

"It seems to me you were her God!" Ken shook his head. "Every man is held accountable for their own choices. We have people and things as our Gods but won't acknowledge God." Ken held his head down in shame. "Listen, Kirk, I will look out for you and your family as long as I can. You, Laura, and Jenny are considered a family now, but after three months it is going to get bad. Do you see how luxurious it is down here, and space is like a rich heaven? Down here is for the middle- and upper-class people. On the other side is where the lower-class people are housed. Some are housed in one room with their families. They are served three meals and two snacks a day like prisoners. Here we can eat what and when we want. We have indoor pools, restaurants, gyms, computers, you name it. The lower class only has pen gyms, and you can forget about restaurants and pools. If your family lives on the poor side, you have to get a pass to visit them. It is the haves and have-nots for now."

"Who is living in space?" Kirk questioned.

"The rich, famous, and government officials." Ken Laughed.

"Then why was I given a choice as to where I wanted my family to go?" Kirk asked sternly clinching his fist.

"I believe it is because you and your family have made quite a name for yourselves, or maybe your friend Bill put in a word for you, I don't know." Ken looked at Kirk with a confused look. "All I know is you had better enjoy it while it lasts," Ken smirked as he showed Kirk to the door. Kirk shook Ken's hand while giving him a side hug, he bid him good night and walked to his apartment.

While walking to his apartment Kirk could not help but notice people smiling and waving as if they were living a good life and all was well. Kirk thought to himself, "Are they crazy, don't they know what is going on?"

Kirk let out a loud grunt as he covered his face with his hands in frustration, "This has never made any atom of sense to me, like I am yet to understand why I have to go through all of this, what for?" He argued with himself as he walked through his apartment door.

"Shhh!" Jenny silently exclaimed as she placed her finger on her mouth, she looked over to Laura who was sleeping, and gestured to Kirk to speak quietly. Kirk tip-toed into the room and stopped beside her, he was careful not to wake Laura up.

"What is going on? Why were you yelling like that?" Jenny asked as she moved over to Laura to pat her gently on her shoulder so that she could keep sleeping.

"So apparently, we have been given three months…," Kirk replied as he collapsed to the bean chair in front of him.

"I don't get it, I don't understand, so please make it crystal clear to me…why have we been given three months? Three months for what exactly?"

"You know that I had to see the officer that has been helping us out ever since we moved into this bunker," Kirk replied as he looked around the apartment.

"And?" Jenny retorted, sounding very impatient, she just wanted to know the truth of what had been going on because she never enjoyed being kept in the dark.

"So, he says… that we have just three months until we have to take the chip…because as it stands, that is the only way that we can keep living in any of their bunkers and getting any money for our upkeep, apparently, it is the only way that we are not going to eventually get killed from all this ruckus happening".

"Are you kidding me right now? Can these people just let us catch a breath, so now what? They are mandating us to take that silly chip, we do not want it, this does not make any sense like a lot has gone so wrong already. I am so confused, I can't deal with their gimmicks anymore," Jenny said as she let out a huge sigh.

"At this point Jenny, we have no other choice…," Kirk replied as he paused to look at Laura, "I have to figure out a way to tell Laura, we both have to figure this out."

"I don't know how we are going to do that, but we just have to figure out a way to do that…we have to find a way to tell her somehow… and I think that you have to be the one to do that," Jenny quirked as she replied.

"I don't know how I am going to tell her…she is already going through so much already as it is, this is all so messed up," Kirk shrieked as he ran his hands through his hair.

"Just breathe Kirk…breathe…it may not look like it now, and I know that none of all that is going on makes any sense…but we are built to overcome everything, we are built to overcome all of this alright? God is with us."

"Oh please, quit the God talk, I am so tired of all that crap already," he replied as he threw his hands in the air in frustration.

"Kirk please calm down, you don't want to wake Laura up in this state please," Jenny said as she attempted to pacify him.

"Just please stop telling me about God…I don't understand why someone everyone keeps saying is so good can do this wickedness against the same people that he claims to love, it is all a mystery to me, it is something I do not think I can handle at the moment, so please do not mention his name any further".

"God is good, and no evil comes from him," Jenny replied as Kirk rolled his eyes in a bid to express his disgust at Jenny's statement.

"Believe me…I am trying so hard to cheer you on and also to believe everything you are saying, but will it also be okay for me to say that I can't seem to bring myself to do that at the moment, or is that me basically pushing for mere luck?"

"Alright, and I am not trying to stop you from expressing your feelings my friend, I just want you to have a little bit of hope especially now that everything seems bleak at the moment" Jenny added, still trying to comfort him.

"I believe that you should just press the brakes on this God talk for now, please. I am not in the mood to get into all that right now. I mean I am the one who literally just got back here from being in a scary conversation with the officer. So, I know that there is no part of all this that can be saved or redeemed" Kirk argued.

"You have to try to keep up hope, even if all seems lost," Jenny replied as she walked to the chair at the other end of the room bunker.

A few minutes later, Laura was woken abruptly from her sleep because of a nightmare that she had, she jerked up from her sleep and slowly began wimping in tears. Kirk rushed over to meet her because Jenny was now fast asleep on the chair at the other end of the room.

"Hey, what is wrong? What happened?" Kirk asked as he went over to see Laura.

"I had a nightmare, Kirk, I had a terrifying nightmare," Laura replied as she rested her head on his shoulder heaving loudly between breaths.

"Do you mind telling me about it?" Kirk said as he stroked her hair trying to calm her down.

"It was a lot Kirk…a lot was happening all at once…it seemed like this whole building was swept away and it put everyone that was seeking refuge here in danger…there were a lot of screams and deep groanings from people who had been in a lot of pain."

"It's okay…it is okay, I'm with you," Kirk responded as he kissed her forehead and stroked her hair again.

Laura noticed Kirk's unusually long silence after she had told him about the nightmare that she had, it was not in his nature to talk too much, but talking about any problems that they had and trying to ease each other's worries was something that they did easily all through the years of their entire relationship and marriage.

She could not stop herself from asking Kirk what the problem was, she looked at him and tried to maintain eye contact but failed in every attempt to do so, "What is wrong with you?"

"Nothing," Kirk said as he tried to look away from her.

"You do know that you are a terrible liar, right?" Laura scoffed as she responded.

"I just told you nothing is wrong," Kirk replied in a soft voice.

"You can't tell me that, I have known you long enough to know when something is wrong, and you can't afford to keep anything from me, not with everything that is going on right now, something's up, I can tell, so could you just spill?" Laura kept insisting.

"I don't know how to say this…" Kirk stopped to look at her, rubbed his neck with his palm, and cleared his throat.

"You don't know how to say what Kirk?"-Laura asked as she started to feel unsettled.

"We have been given three months, Babe" Kirk finally spoke up.

"I don't get you, what have we been given three months for?" Laura hesitantly responded.

"We have been given three months to get the chip," Kirk blurted out as he held Laura's hand.

"Whattttttt? What do you mean by that? How did you get to know? What does that mean?" Laura quizzed Kirk while trying to retain her balance.

"Whoa, babe...slow down, will you calm down?"

"No Kirk, I obviously can't slow down, tell me...how did you get to know?"

"I just got back from seeing the officer...the one that has been helping us ever since we got to this bunker, we had a long conversation, and he explained everything to me, he said the government is going to be giving all the people that have not gotten the chip yet, three months to do so...so as it is, we either have to either get the chip to survive while we are here, or we risk losing our lives".

Laura quivered as soon as Kirk finished speaking, "But you know that is not an option, right? we can't get the chip, I hope you are not thinking about getting it..."

"I don't know baby, I am so confused right now, I don't know what to think or do."

"Getting the chip is not an option...we know more than anyone else what getting the chip would mean for our lives going forward," Laura replied, getting a little too agitated.

"Baby please could we not argue about this right now, let's not start a fight, it is not what we need, we just have to figure a way out of all this."

"I don't see any other way out of this, we have only five hundred dollars, I don't know how we are going to survive with that amount of money for the next three months, I don't know how it is going to work."

"I can't believe you; I can't believe that you are honestly thinking about getting the chip…you are so unbelievable."

"Look babe…I do not want to get stressed out over this issue, so please can we just drop it?"

"Wow Kirk…just wow, I have nothing to say to you until you come back to your senses," Laura huffed as she angrily looked at her husband.

"What do you want me to do babe…I am helpless and clueless here…it's not just us involved remember? Hundreds of people that are also seeking refuge here are also affected, so it is not in my hands to make any decisions, I am not the government," Kirk replied as he walked to the small fridge in front of him to get a glass of water.

"What's going on with you two?" Jenny said as she sluggishly stood up from the chair on which she was previously asleep.

"Did you hear about the government wanting to give us the chip?" Laura asked Jenny as she watched her stretch out her arms.

"Unfortunately, yes, I did…Kirk told me about it as soon as he came back to the bunker after speaking with the officer, you were asleep then, so I did not want to wake you up," Jenny responded.

"Tell me honestly…does any of that make any sense to you? I mean the government mandating us to take the chip against our will is just simply outrageous," Laura barked.

"You just need to relax okay…I agree with you, but I don't want to take the chip because I know exactly what it means, but all I can do now is just hope for the best possible outcome from all this," Kirk said, trying to calm her down.

"Enough of the hope talk…this is not a façade, it is our current reality, we could die, there is a high possibility that we are not making it out alive, so please do not talk to me about hope" Laura argued.

"I'm sorry…just relax okay, please this is not good for your health, you only just started recovering, please take it easy."

"I am not in the right state of mind, I do not need this right now, you do not have to tell me about hope because I have lost every ounce of it," Laura remarked.

"My friend…I am so sorry, please relax, okay? try not to dwell on this please," Jenny said as she stroked Laura's back.

"Baby please, think about your health, okay? "We will try not to talk about the chip for as long as we can," Kirk said as he tried to embrace Laura.

"Can he just take us already? I am so tired of it all, so can he just take us all and put us out of this misery?" Laura screamed as Kirk struggled to hold her down.

"Please do not say that Laura, please take it easy, remember you are not fully recovered yet," Jenny said and offered her a cup of water.

Laura angrily shrugged Jenny's hands off as she brought the cup of water close to her which resulted in the glass breaking as soon as it hit the wall of the bunker.

"Oh my God Laura! calm down!" Jenny shrieked as she stepped back to look around so that she would be sure that the glass did not hit any part of her body, she looked at Kirk and also examined him. She saw that he had a cut on his wrist and tried taking Laura to another side of the room.

"Do not tell me to calm down, don't tell me to calm down," Laura replied amidst shedding very strong tears.

"Kirk was hurt…we have to clean his wound up, Kirk come and sit here," Jenny said as she pointed Kirk towards the chair. She went around the bunker searching for a first aid kit and some minutes after, she walked back into the room holding a small white box.

"Hey Kirk, we just need to dress the wound to stop the bleeding, so please try to stay still while I do just that," Jenny said as she grabbed some cotton wool and spirit from the first aid box and started cleaning up the wound.

After a few minutes, Jenny finished cleaning his wound and moved on to cover up the wound and wrap it up with a band aid and finally a bandage just so the wound could heal properly, "All done," she said as she lightly tapped Kirk's wrist.

"Thank you so much Jenny," Kirk said as he smiled and thanked her.

"You are welcome," Jenny replied.

"Please could you also help me talk to Laura, she seems to be raving these days, and I understand that, given everything she has gone through all this time, but I just need her to take things easy, so she does not spiral out of control."

Jenny sighed and lightly patted Kirk on his shoulder before she replied, "I am so sorry for everything that just happened Kirk…we both know that Laura isn't usually like this, and quite frankly, all that she has experienced is enough to break someone…so we can't blame her for her actions, all we can do for her right now is be there, but don't you worry, I will try to talk to her and hopefully, she listens to me, again I am so sorry Kirk, believe me, none of us have to go through all these things".

"Please do, I am out of options already, I am really worried about her, and I do not know what to do anymore," Kirk replied as he lowered his face to express his sadness.

"I will just try to take some rest, okay? I'll be back to check on you," Jenny said and went over to meet Laura.

Jenny went over to sit with Laura, she looked at her and tried to keep eye contact, but it was not possible because Laura was too phased out to notice that Jenny had been sitting beside her.

"Laura, what was that about? Why did you have to react like that, what is wrong?"

After a few minutes of trying to speak with Laura, Jenny resolved that it was better to just leave her by herself until she was eventually ready to talk. She stroked Laura's hair and tried walking away when she heard soft whimpers behind her, she turned around and saw Laura weeping profusely, so much so that her hair started getting soaked from the tears.

She ran back to her and embraced her after she noticed that Kirk had gone into the other room to take a nap, "It's okay…it's okay, please it's okay."

"No, it's not, no it's not okay…," Laura replied while struggling to stop herself from crying any louder, "My babies…they did not deserve any of this, they did not deserve this kind of treatment."

"They are in a much better place now Laura, I know that it sucks… being away from them, and I would be lying if I said I understand what you are going through, but listen…", Jenny said as she raised Laura's head and tried to clean her eyes, "I am here for you…Kirk is here for you, we are both here for you and we want to help you…so please let us". Jenny's outpour was met with much stronger walls than the previous, at this point she felt that all she could do was just be there to hold her, and to allow them both to enjoy some form of silence, as telling her anything or trying to console her was no longer working, she just knew that she had to be there for her friend even if it meant sitting in silence for a couple of minutes without saying a word.

Chapter Fourteen

Kirk could not get a minute's sleep the previous night, he kept moving around the bed because not only was he in a lot of pain as a result of his heavily bandaged wrist. He also had a lot of things on his mind, which was very unsettled ever since he finished the conversation, he had had with Officer Ken the previous day.

He had not quite gotten over the conflicting feeling of having to take the chip, or rather being mandated by the government to take the chip, and about their future afterward. He was also a little bit shaken up by the argument he had with Laura, and they had also not resolved their conflict or attempted to talk about it because Laura did not speak to him all through the night.

"Hey babe," Kirk said as he propped himself up on the bed and gently tapped Laura's shoulder, she had her back facing him because she was still not in the mood to speak with him.

"What?" Laura replied angrily without turning to face him.

"Can we please talk?" Kirk asked as he placed his hand on her waist.

"I am not in the mood, I do not want to talk to you," Laura replied as she shrugged his hand off from her waist.

"Babe please, you know I cannot handle when you are like this? This is the last thing that we need at the moment," Kirk replied as he tried to get Laura's attention.

"Kirk please could you do me a favor? Leave me alone, okay? Please just let me be."

"You know fully well that I cannot do that babe," Kirk responded as he placed his hand on her waist again.

Laura let out a loud grunt in frustration as she sat up on the bed, "you want to talk right? Okay then, let us talk, are you thinking about getting the chip?"

Kirk took a deep breath in before he replied, "Babe, you know fully well that it is beyond me, I do not have a choice at this point, we do not have a choice, it's basically going to be what our future is going to be in the next three months. I do not have the final say in all of this, please just try to understand."

"Wow, in all of the years that we have been together, this is probably the first time that I am going to admit that I do not know who is sitting across from me right now because it is certainly not the man that I married," Laura replied angrily.

"Please just try to reason with me, I am out of options here," Kirk said as he took Laura's hands.

"You have clearly shown me that there is no point in reasoning or attempting to reason with you, I don't know why you would even think about doing that, it is all beyond me," Laura shrieked as she stood up from the bed and walked to the bathroom.

A few minutes later, she walked back in with a towel wrapped around her hair. She walked over to the corner of the room where they kept the boxes that held their clothes and she reached to get a gown. Jenny walked into their room and noticed the cold aura that covered the room. She was in utter disbelief that they had allowed anger and a lot of mixed emotions to spill over from the previous day.

"Kirk…Laura, I would like to have a word with the two of you, come with me, let's go to the main room," Jenny said and left the room.

They both exchanged glances at each other with Laura still being visibly angry before following Jenny to the other room.

Before settling down in front of her, they kept holding their straight and unamused faces and expressions. Jenny proceeded to speak, "I was going to start by asking how your night went if you slept well and all of that but judging from the look on your faces…I can tell and also sense that there is still a lot of tension from the argument that you had yesterday."

"I would not be a good friend to the both of you if I said that I liked the way that things have been carrying on with the both of you, particularly since the moment that we moved into this bunker. It has been extremely hard for me to watch the two of you tear each other apart because of everything that has happened in the last few days, and I must say that I am not happy at all. The incessant fights and quarrels are starting to get to me, and I want to please beg you to sort things out."

Kirk looked at Laura and walked to meet her where she was sitting, "I am sorry baby. I am sorry if any of my actions have hurt or upset you in the last few days. It was not my intention. I just want to let you know that I am here for you no Michaeler what, through all this craziness happening. I don't like it when we fight, it is the one thing that I cannot stand, it is something that always irks me. We have been through a lot of ups and downs, and most recently only downs for you to think or assume that I am not on your side through all of this, that alone really hurts me."

Laura turned to face him just so their eyes met, she held his hand and for the first time in a while, she saw someone other than herself, she saw the man that she had vowed to spend the rest of her life with, the one she had promised her love, honor, and respect to through all the years, she felt sorry that she blamed him for wanting to take the chip, after all, like he said, it was not up to him.

"I am the one who is sorry baby, I do not know what came over me. I never should have lashed out at you like that or blamed you, I guess I had been so overwhelmed with different emotions from everything that has been happening. I never should have taken out my frustration on you, I should have let you know how I felt, I should have talked my feelings out with you," Laura responded as she took his hands and stroked them, she tearfully looked at him as they exchanged a few kisses.

Jenny clasped her hands together as she jumped in excitement, "Yaya, now that is more like it, there you go, finally some peace and quiet," she said as she rolled her eyes sarcastically and Kirk and Laura laughed loudly at her statement and mannerisms. "While we are still stuck here, can I beg you two, or rather ask you for a favor…please do not bite each other's heads off, I think I am finally at my wit's end from watching the two of you argue non-stop these last few days", Jenny said as she quirkily smiled at Kirk and Laura.

"We will try not to," Kirk and Laura both responded in unison as they laughed again at what Jenny said. They later decided that they were going to do everything to enjoy what they felt was going to be their very last days on earth as the ultimatum for them getting the chip as mandated by the government drew near.

They were in a queue at the general store in the underground facility as they went to shop for some food supplies, Kirk had thought that they could all go indulge themselves in a fun activity and he thought of going to take a dive in the indoor pool and that he was going to ask Laura and Jenny to accompany him as he felt that it was something that they all needed.

"Hey babe…," he said as he reluctantly asked Laura because he was not sure of what her response was going to be, "Would you like to go swimming."

Laura beamed with excitement while she scanned the shelves at the store and jumped in excitement as she hugged him, "Just what I need, of course, I would like to go swimming."

"Do you care to ask Jenny, I just felt like we have not had something like this in a long while, so it would be good for all of us," Kirk said as he smiled broadly at Laura.

"Okay, I will ask her," Laura replied as she excitedly skipped to meet Jenny, "Hi Jenny, Kirk says to ask you if you would like to go swimming in the indoor pool, we need this you know? To take the edge off."

"Yes, I would love to go swimming with your knuckleheads," Jenny hilariously responded.

"Cool, then we are going swimming," Laura said as she took Jenny's hands, and they went back to meet Kirk.

After they got back to their bunker, Kirk thought to check their credit balance and saw that they had a hundred and fifty dollars left to spend, he wondered how it was going to be enough for them to be able to get more supplies in the long run, but he did not want to bother Laura or Jenny about it.

They left their bunker and walked to the indoor pool of the underground facility to take a swim like they had earlier agreed, they walked in and saw some people lounging around the pool, it seemed as if they were not going through the same things that Kirk and Laura had gone through, or maybe they just chose to be oblivious in that moment.

Laura was inspired by the beaming smiles and echoing laughter that they resolved to, "These people act like nothing's wrong, and it is inspiring to watch," she whispered to Kirk as they walked to the other side of the pool while Jenny led them.

As they dipped their bodies into the pool, Kirk took a second look at the people facing them on the other side of the pool. Laura was right, these people that he watched closely were admirable, they acted like the world as they knew it was not going to come to an end anytime soon, he had been so lost in thoughts that he didn't feel Laura splashing water on him. "Kirk!" she called out to him as she splashed some more later on his face, he smiled shortly and kissed her forehead.

Just a few minutes later, the speakerphones on the walls surrounding the indoor pool came on, "Good day all, this is just to inform us, that there will be a nationwide address in a few minutes, and we are going to be addressed by the President, please stay tuned as we expect this broadcast."

"Good day, citizens of America…", the president's voice filled the room as it abruptly became silent, "I bring you good news, one that would benefit the great people and nation of America as a whole, it is my pleasure to announce that we have found the Messiah, the one that we have identified as been able to heal the sick and cure both the named and the unnamed diseases we have plaguing our beloved and blessed nation, he shall be called Ultimo, and it is to him that you now owe all form of allegiance and obedience to".

"We believe that he is here for such a time as this to bring peace and relief to our distorted world, so I want to urge us all to surrender and bow to him. I want to state that it is very important that you worship and bow to him at all times, bow and worship him whenever he speaks or utters any word, or makes any declarations or risk being put to death, if you default in any of these commands, you are at risk of losing your life".

"Please be duly warned that Ultimo is who we now regard as our Savior and no other god can be equaled with him, no one should be found, seen, or heard regarding any other master and savior aside Ultimo for any reason because effective from today, he is now regarded as the only messiah of the people and nation of America from now henceforth".

After the announcement, everyone was in shock that no one wanted to swim anymore. Everyone jumped out of the pool, dried off, and went back to their bunker.

Chapter Fifteen

Both Kirk and Laura were unable to sleep that night. As he noticed her moving restlessly on the bed, he grabbed her and held her tight. Laura just sobbed and cried. "thou shall have no other God before me, I am the way, the truth, and the light." Laura muttered to herself. "I will not worship this ULTIMO!" Tears started to roll down Kirk's face, and he tried to catch them before they fell so Laura wouldn't notice him weeping.

"Babe try to calm down, I hear someone at the door," Kirk whispered as he rose out of bed to see who it was. Before his feet could touch the floor, Jenny had already answered the door. "Kirk, it is Ken."

"Ken, I am glad you are here," Kirk said hesitantly.

"Listen Kirk very carefully, we do not have much time. Your friend Bill sent me a message yesterday via email stating he would like to see you. I quickly erased it because those who are in space are not supposed to communicate with anyone other than officials. Bill will be arriving soon." Officer McCauley, stated. "If he has chosen to live in space, how can he travel here?" Kirk asked in confusion.

"For three months some people will be able to travel back and forth to help convince their friends and family to take the chip. He was given a pass to come and see me. He will have an escort with him who will wait for him in the communal area. I will let you know when Bill arrives." Officer McCauley stated as he opened the door to leave. Two hours had passed, then three hours. Kirk, Laura, and Jenny were getting anxious.

They sat in silence anticipating Bill's arrival. Finally, there was a knock at the door. It was Officer McCauley coming to take Kirk to his place.

"Wait here, I will be back soon." Kirk kissed Laura on the cheek and looked at Jenny while he nodded his head at her.

Ken and Kirk walked down the hall to his bunker where Bill was waiting inside. As soon as Ken opened the door, Bill reached past him and grabbed Kirk.

"How are you, man?" Bill grinned.

Kirk failed to reply.

"Okay just listen, I have a plan for you and your family." Bill handed Kirk a map. Kirk shook his head in disgust.

"No one uses maps anymore, haven't you heard of GPS?" Kirk frowned.

"Come on man use your head, tracker," Bill said sternly. "Just listen. I have a place in Alabama, a house on a field surrounded by land. There is an underground bunker full of supplies. In fact, there are several buildings with underground bunkers and places to hide. Ultimo is in charge now. People are living in space drinking and partying and saying hail to their king. There is no sickness there. Everyone is well. Those who were ill are now well. There is no age limit there, people are committing sexual acts that you would consider Haynes. Kirk, you, and your family will find your fate soon if you do not leave this place. I know you are not going to take the chip." Bill said as he held his head down. Officer McCauley interrupted, "I have agreed to escort you there. I will plan an accident with a commotion, leaving a suicide note stating I cannot allow my family to live this way and I just want to die. We will escape tonight." Ken looked at Kirk with wide eyes.

"IT WILL NOT WORK, I REPEAT, WILL NOT WORK! They will look for us." Kirk yelled.

"Trust me there are only two officers on this side including myself and Officer Bryon, You will start a fire in your apartment, I will disguise myself and escort everyone out of the building," Ken assured Kirk. When Officer Bryon arrives, he will be worried about making sure everyone is safe. When he checks my bunker, he will find a suicide note stating I have killed myself and my family and set your bunker with your family on fire. He will only find ashes in your place, and no one in my place at all. He will report to all officials that something tragic has happened and we have lost two families. We will be long gone by then trust me, Kirk. It will take us two hours to get to Alabama from here in North Carolina. Go now and prepare your family to leave, take nothing with you. Burn some of your clothes and put the fire out. Then when we are headed out, I will have everyone evacuated while you set the real fire. There is an old plane full of fuel about a mile away. We will walk there and take off tonight headed to Alabama." Officer McCauley explained as he shook hands with Bill thanking him.

Bill bid everyone Farwell because he knew he would never see them again. He quietly walked to the spacecraft that was waiting for him in the next parking lot. When he got to the ship, the officer waiting patted him on the back.

"No luck, you did not get your family to agree to get the chip?" the officer asked him.

"No sir," Bill responded

As they began to descend into the air, they saw a big ball of smoke coming from one side of the bunker. Bill held his stomach and gasped for air.

"Shall I turn around?" The officer said with concern.

"No, there is nothing we can do," Bill forced a tear out of his eye, because he knew exactly what was going on. He did a good job holding in his excitement knowing everything was going as planned.

Kirk rushed to the bunker and put all their clothes together so that he could set them on fire as they had discussed, a part of him had been extremely nervous because he knew that what they were about to do was extremely risky, he was not willing to put his and his family's life at risk, so getting them out of the facility safely was all he could think about in that moments.

He paced around the corner of the room that he was standing in and took a few short breaths before he could get a grip on himself again. He grabbed a matchbox, put all the clothes together, and lit a fire on them. Once he saw the fire building, he ran out of the bunker and ran over to where Jenny, Laura, and Officer Ken had been waiting.

"Hurry, Hurry! we need to leave right now," Officer Ken said as he led his family, Kirk, Laura, and Jenny out of the facility as it had already been fully engulfed in flames.

"We don't have so much time…oh Lord! I am so scared," Laura shrieked as Kirk held her hands as Jenny led her into the heavily guarded and bulletproof van that they all had to enter to seek safety. Kirk and Laura held hands with Jenny as she prayed while the van swerved around to be able to successfully leave the facility.

Meanwhile, at the facility, Officer Byron and another officer walked towards the bunker that belonged to Kirk and his family, the others had been fully occupied with trying to get to a safer part of the facility that was not so affected by the fire that had erupted.

"Oh my God!" Officer Byron screamed as they reached the entrance of Kirk's bunker, they had all worn protective suits and oxygen masks to protect themselves from the uproar that the fire had caused, "no one should go in…," Officer Byron screamed as he peeked into the bunker through a window that was by the wall.

"it seems like there is no one here, I can't hear any voices or screams, so it is possible that they might have disappeared or something," Officer

Byron said as he gave the other officer a long pat on his back as they walked away from the bunker and ran into the facility's main hall.

As they walked back into the passage leading to the main hall, Officer Byron stopped in his tracks as he looked up at the other officer that was with him, he noticed that he had not seen Officer Ken all through the period of the outbreak of the fire at the facility and also while the other officers had been trying to move everyone in the facility that were affected by the fire in one way or another to safety.

"Hey, have you seen Officer Ken?" Officer Byron asked.

"No, I have not seen him. In fact, I have not seen him since we had breakfast together this morning," the officer replied as he shook his head.

"Then we have to go and look for him and we have to hurry, let us go and check his bunker," Officer Byron said as they ran through the main hallway of the facility to Officer Ken's bunker.

When they got there, Officer Byron noticed that the bunker had not been affected by the fire yet, so he decided that he would go in to check for Officer Ken or any of his family members.

After searching the bunker for about three minutes, he did not see anyone, he was about to step out of the bunker when he saw a piece of paper on the floor, he picked it up and began to read the content of the paper out loud. "To whom it may concern, by the time you will be reading this, I would have been dead…I decided to save myself from the extended misery of what is to come as my heart can no longer bear any form of heartache or pain… Before I thought of doing this, I had thought it through, and I could not help but be filled with regrets that this was what I had to come to for me to finally be at peace again. I tried…I tried to be strong and fight off this thought for so many weeks, but I guess that this was the most logical thing to do because I cannot bear this pain any longer…

I apologize if this would make any one of you sad, my colleagues, friends, or anyone that I deemed to be very dear to me and close to my heart, I did not mean to cause you any pain, I just had to do this for me. I appreciate everyone who has helped me throughout my lifetime on this earth, and particularly I want to thank my fellow officers in service who have displayed an enviable amount of bravery in ensuring the safety of everyone in these dark times that we are facing.

I write this letter with deep sorrow and regret in my heart, but I cannot face or bear anything that is worse than the current. I cannot find the strength in me to do so…and that is the reason why I had to do this, in the most peaceful manner and just because I felt like it is the most reasonable thing for me to do at this juncture…I also want to say that or rather apologize for one other thing…I have unnecessarily taken life into my own hands…

I am deeply sorry, but I killed Kirk, alongside his wife and their longtime friend that they have been staying with ever since they got into this facility. The reason why I did that was because I really felt like they were not appreciative enough, they did not appreciate my efforts in trying to keep them safe in all the crisis and chaos happening around us, and so I just had to kill them all. I hope that probably if there is another life apart from this one, they can learn from their mistakes, and learn to be more thankful and show gratitude for people's efforts towards them.

Once again, I am terribly sorry for the pain that this may cause to anyone who is reading this or to anyone that this news may get to in the long run, please forgive me. I did not mean to cause you any harm or pain, please do not be sorrowful or sad about what I did, carry on with your lives or what is left of it and try to soak in every passing moment. I am incredibly grateful for my time here and the impact that I have made in the lives of other people and our dear country, and you should be too, Till we meet again, Ken."

"Oh my God! a complete rascal until the very end," Officer Byron screeched as he squeezed the piece of paper in his hands and then threw it against the wall as he clenched his fist and punched it on the wall so much that his knuckles started bleeding.

"What is it? What happened?" The other officer said as he ran into the room that Officer Byron was in, he rushed over to him when he saw blood trickling down to the floor from his knuckles.

"That rascal killed himself! Can you just imagine that? That is just ridiculous," Officer Byron said as he held his knuckle and tried to stop blood from spilling to the floor any further.

"Woah, how could he do that? That is just crazy! Why would he think of doing that though?" The other officer replied screaming at the top of his lungs.

"I really don't know man…it's annoying that he thought that this was the right way to end things," Officer Byron said, gripping his hand firmly and writhing in pain.

"Alright, we just have to get you cleaned up as soon as possible…"

"Is everyone safe? Hope no one is still around the affected area of the fire outbreak," Officer Byron asked as his partner led him out into the hallway. He kept thinking of Officer Ken. They had joined the network together and practically built their lives outside the work they did together as well, he could not believe that he would have thought about taking his own life.

Kirk, Officer Ken, and their families had struggled so much to get to safety that they would be able to board the plane that was waiting at the hangar to take them to safety. They were very anxious because they had to escape that night so that no one would identify them or be able to find out where they were.

Officer Ken had promised Bill that he was going to do everything in his power to ensure that Kirk and his family were safe, and he also secretly wished that the officers back at the government underground facility would have been a part of their plan. He did not believe that he would have to fake his own death to be able to protect his family and secure the lives of some other people, people he had grown fonder of after interaction.

Kirk held Laura's hand tightly when he noticed that she had begun to hyperventilate; they had been in an enclosed area for a while in a tinted and bulletproof van. Officer Ken had suggested that they hide in an enclosed uncompleted building's compound, one that not many people knew of, and they would not be searching or stamping through, at least for the time being that they were going to be in there.

"Are you okay babe?" Kirk asked as he looked intently at Laura. Jenny noticed that Laura had been struggling hard to breathe, she went over to her side and tried to release the buttons of the gown that she had on, "Please can we have the windows opened?" Jenny asked as she looked around the van.

"We can't," Officer Ken replied as he clasped his hands and looked at Jenny sternly.

"Why can't we open the windows, I am sure you can see what is going on right now…," Jenny said as she gestured to Laura, "she needs some air."

"I don't know if you are living under a rock or just trying to be annoying on purpose but…we are hiding, one little slip-up could give us away within the snap of a finger or a few seconds, and the windows are going to remain closed," Officer Ken thundered.

Kirk rolled his eyes at the abysmal display of negligence between Officer Ken and Jenny, and he was starting to get extremely fed up, "Guys, my wife is fighting for her life over here!" he said as he pointed at Laura as she rested her head on his shoulder struggling in between breaths.

"Can we just have one of the windows opened for about five minutes please?" Kirk asked as he looked at Officer Ken.

"Alright fine…but just know that we can't be here forever, we still have to leave tonight."

"I hear you Ken, but we are talking about my wife here, so please just open one of the windows, and once she is stable, we will restart our journey," Kirk quaked as he responded.

"Fine," Officer Ken said as he gestured to one of the officers escorting them to open up one of the windows.

After a few minutes, Officer Ken asked for the windows to be closed so they could continue their journey to the hangar where they were going to board the plane to go to Bill's underground bunker in Alabama. "Hi Laura, I hope that you are doing much better now?" he asked as he walked over to where Laura was sitting to check on her.

"I don't know how I feel," Laura replied faintly as she looked up to see Officer Ken's face.

"Not to worry, you are going to be alright, you are going to be just fine, okay?" he said as he reassuringly looked at Laura as Kirk stroked her hair so that she could go to sleep.

"Thank you," Kirk whispered as he thanked Officer Ken and looked up to see Jenny smiling at him, so he returned the smile.

After a half-hour drive, they finally got to the hangar that housed the airplane that they were going to use to get to Alabama. Officer Ken took it upon himself to immediately start ushering the people out of the van and safely into the bus, "Alright guys, we have to get going now, it is best we start our journey now so we can get to Alabama before sunrise, so please get your things and let us start going now, thank you all for your understanding and your cooperation, I really appreciate it".

Laura and Jenny were fast asleep by the time they got onto the bus aside from Officer Ken's wife, daughter, and the other officer who was escorting them. Kirk was also wide awake throughout the journey when he noticed the plane a few steps away from where the van that they were in was parked. He felt a deep sense of relief that they were at least able to get to the hangar safely and sound without any complications or avoidable issues.

"Hey guys…hey," Kirk said as he tried to wake Laura and Jenny up from their sleep. They both stretched as they tried to sit up and look around.

"We are here, we are at the hangar, let us go," Kirk said as he tilted his head and gestured to Laura and Jenny. Jenny stood up and helped Kirk with getting Laura out of the van and into the plane. After a few minutes of onboarding, Officer Ken waved to his subordinate officer, "Hey, now that everyone is settled, can you help me out with checking the fuel tank of the plane so that I can know if we have just enough fuel in there that can take us safely to Alabama."

The officer nodded as he went down to go and check the fuel pump of the plane and do some last-minute checks on the plane.

He came back a few minutes later while adjusting his buckle, he looked up and saluted Officer Ken, "It is all clear sir."

"All clear?" Officer Ken replied to be sure of what the officer said.

The officer nodded as he replied again, "Yes sir, it is all clear. I checked the fuel pump of the plane like you asked me to and we have enough fuel there that is certainly going to safely take us to Alabama," he said as he saluted Officer Ken again.

"Okay, thank you very much," he said as he patted the officer lightly on his shoulder.

"Alright now, let us get ready for our journey," Officer Ken said as he clapped his hands to get everyone's attention and then made his way to the cockpit of the plane so that he could control it since they had no pilot.

After about two hours, they finally got out of the plane and drove to Bill's hidden safety bunker. Officer Ken was happy that he was able to get them settled in the bunker before sunrise as he had wished. "Alright, everyone, we are finally here guys, thankfully we were able to get to this place just in time with no hassles, so let us all just settle in and all try to lay very low for the time being."

Kirk got up to help Laura out as she was still very weak, he walked her to the front porch and entrance of the underground bunker, he shook hands with Officer Ken and they both shared a side hug, "Thank you so much for doing this for all of us, we are grateful, my family and I are so grateful, you have no idea, it means so much to me that you are always particular about the safety of others".

"You are welcome, Kirk," Officer Ken said as he tapped Kirk's shoulder and gave him a reassuring nod.

They walked into the bunker and Officer Ken assigned their rooms to them. After they rested for a couple of minutes, the officer called them all for a brief meeting. "Hi everyone, I would want to start by asking how we all are doing, but I know the answers are only going to be farfetched, the reason being that we have been going through a series of hardships over the past few weeks, and at this point, hope might not be achievable or even attained, I just want to assure you that we are all going to go through the rest of these hard days together. We all must be a united front in these days ahead, and I mean that with all sense of sincerity. I want our sense of togetherness to be strengthened more than ever before...," he looked around before he was able to continue speaking again, "Thankfully, through the help of one of my friends who is currently being housed in outer space, we were able to get to this secret underground bunker for safety. At least I know that all of us here are certainly not going to be getting the chip that the government proposed for us to be able to sustain our lives here. I am sure that our refusal to take the chip is going to cause a lot of uproar amongst people, but thankfully as it stands, no one knows where we are, and I think they would not suspect anything at the moment because I had to fake my own death and also lie that I murdered Kirk and his family. However, we must all ensure that we keep a low profile while we are in here, for now, I have looked around to ensure that this bunker is safe and equally secure for all, we have food supplies that should last us for the next couple of days or weeks while we are here, no one must step out of this bunker at any point in time, I repeat no one must leave this bunker at any time. We do not want to easily give ourselves away, at any point, if you need anything, please do not hesitate to let me know, I will try to satisfy your wants in my capacity if need be.

So please let us all ensure that our stay here is one that is peaceful and without any unnecessary mishaps whatsoever, if you are uncomfortable or seem to be unpleasant about something then I should reiterate that you should please voice your opinions to me and not any other person living here. While we are here, I am also going to serve as your pastor. We will gather regularly and pray together from time to time, it is because of him…," he paused and pointed to the ceiling, "that we are even still alive in the first place."

"I do not care about no God! What kind of God forsakes the ones that love him and neglects them at their point of need and in their disappointments," Laura yelled out.

"Laura please try to get a hold of yourself, please do not speak ill of God, no Michaeler what he is still god," Officer Ken responded.

"You know what, I am just about done with God! He does not care about me, he never did, and he is so wicked," Laura shrieked as she yelled at Officer Ken.

"Hey Laura," Kirk said as he crouched in front of her, "You really need to lie down, okay? You need to calm down please; it is not good for you."

"Leave me alone, I am not interested in all of this, I want out, I am miserable already, so if he will just hurry it up and take my life like he always wanted to, that would be nice," Laura yelled out again.

"Alright Laura, that is enough, you need to go and rest, you need to go and lie down now," Jenny said assisting her withstanding up and also leading her into the inner quarters of the bunker where their bedrooms were.

Jenny led Laura to the bed, and she tried to calm her down before she could fall asleep, "Listen, Laura, the way that you are going about this is seriously not the best. Please try to be calmer. I have told you over and over again that lashing out like this is not the best for you, particularly when you are like this and also with your state of health. Please I know it is extremely hard to do that right now, but we have no choice."

"I am so tired of everyone talking about taking it easy or calming down, it only triggers me further, and I no longer want any part of it, can't you see that? Can't he just end all this now? Like I have had enough misery that could last me my whole lifetime" Laura said in despair.

"Alright, you need to calm down now, try and get some sleep okay?" Jenny responded as she stroked Laura's hair and she fell asleep.

A few minutes later, Jenny walked into the main lounge of the bunker, and she found Kirk lying down on one of the chairs in the lounge, "she is asleep now, thank God! I just hope she did not cause any trouble for you and Officer Ken, where is he by the way?"

"He just stepped into his room, he said that he wanted to take a short nap, thankfully, he was not upset, he said he understood what she was going through. I do not know what to do anymore…I …hate to see her like this…I do not know what to do," Kirk said as he covered his face and started crying profusely.

"Hey…Heyyy, it's okay," Jenny said as she walked over to Kirk to console him and stop him from crying, "it is just a phase, she is going to be okay, she is going to be just fine, she is a fighter, and you know this. This will all be over soon, so try not to hurt yourself so that you do not get sick, Laura needs you at the moment."

"I just want her to be okay, I hate seeing her like this, it hurts to see her like this," Kirk added.

"I know, but all we can do is just be there for her and rally around her now, that is basically a bulk of what she needs, knowing and seeing that there are still a few people left who care about her and want her to be okay", Jenny said as she stroked his shoulder and looked at him reassuringly. "You know what? I think we should all just go and rest, it has been such a long day and the journey getting here definitely was not an easy one.

"Alright, I do not feel like sleeping at all, but I will just take your advice and go in to take some rest because I think that is the best thing to do at the moment."

The next few hours after they had all gone in to take a rest all went by so quickly, Officer Ken had announced that they should all come together to have dinner at the main lounge's leisure area of the bunker, they all gathered and picked up the food of choice before they started eating.

A few minutes after they started having dinner, Laura started getting uncomfortable, she dropped her spoon and started throwing up her food. Kirk rushed over to her and offered her a glass of warm water to drink, she instantly started choking, Jenny ran over to her side to check on her and saw that she was that she was hyperventilating again and this time it was much worse than the first time it happened which was in less than forty-eight hours.

"Please do we have any oxygen masks lying around here, please can someone just quickly help me to get one?" Jenny yelled out as she looked around them. The other officer with them scrambled out of the lounge area to go and search for any oxygen masks in the storage area of the bunker.

Kirk held Laura's hand and tried to make her sit up, but the hyperventilation had gotten much worse than when it started a few minutes ago, "Baby please, stay with me okay, look at me", Kirk said as he tried to make Laura look at him, he was trying to maintain their eye contact.

The officer came back a few minutes later and shook his head as his eyes met Jenny's, "I am sorry, I searched everywhere but I could not find an oxygen mask, I scrambled through every room in the bunker."

"Oh my God! this is just so ridiculous, of all things not to have in this bunker, it's an oxygen mask for crying out loud!" Jenny looked at Laura and tried to resuscitate her, she kept trying without noticing that everyone in the bunker stared intently at her.

She sighed after a while and examined Laura for a pulse and heartbeat, but she did not find one. She had feared that the worst possible thing that she could have ever imagined would have happened, she tried to hope that what she was suddenly nursing was not the case and she also struggled not to let fear overwhelm her.

She stood up from Laura's side and sighed again as she regained her balance, "What is it?" Kirk yelled out as he looked at her, she sighed as she placed her hands on Kirk's shoulder, "I am so sorry Kirk, she has left us, she is no longer with us," she said as she struggled to control herself and stop herself from crying.

"What do you mean she is gone? She can't be gone," he knelt down beside Laura's lifeless body and began to cry uncontrollably, just then they heard the door of the bunker come open all of a sudden, and all of them stopped in their tracks in shock.

"Everyone freeze!" a voice filled the room as two officers entered the bunker and began to search them for the chip that the government had asked everyone to get, anyone without a chip was shot immediately. One of the officers saw Officer Ken, "What are you doing here traitor?" Before Ken could say a word, he shot him in the head execution style. Jenny screamed historically and fainted. An officer sprayed bullets into her while she lay on the floor. Then he stopped in front of Kirk who was holding Laura in his arms, and as he attempted to shoot him, Kirk yelled out in pain, "For God, I live and For God I die Jesus is my savior and my God!

Thank you for your support.

Please make sure you write a review on Amazon and Barnes and Noble, or wherever you purchase your book. This will help the author get recognized on the best Author list.

Please follow Author Felice on Facebook, Groups on Facebook, #rspbooksandmorebooks,

Twitter, and Instagram

Email: Author for mentorship and publishing at

rightsideceo@yahoo.com